DEATH BY INVITATION

SERIES BY NELLIE H. STEELE

Cate Kensie Mysteries

Shadow Slayers Stories

Lily & Cassie by the Sea Mysteries

Great Maine Mysteries

Pearl Party Mysteries

Middle Age is Murder Cozy Mysteries

Duchess of Blackmoore Mysteries

Shadow Lake Ranch Murders

Maggie Edwards Adventures

Clif & Ri on the Sea Adventures

Shelving Magic

Affair with Hair Cozy Mysteries

DEATH BY INVITATION

NELLIE H. STEELE

PROLOGUE

I - KELLY

Kelly stirred the vegetables sautéing in the pan absentmindedly as she stared into space. Only the sharp scream of the smoke alarm drew her attention away from her worried thoughts.

She snapped her gaze down to the now-burned peppers and onions with a grimace before she grabbed her dish towel and waved it at the alarm in a desperate attempt to stop its screeching.

As it finally ceased its incessant shouting, she grabbed the pan from the cooktop and dumped it in the sink.

The letter she received earlier had ruined her meal. And she loved to cook. Except today. Not after receiving the letter.

She wrinkled her nose as the scent of burned vegetables filled the air. She turned on the faucet, drowning them with water to cover the smell before she rifled through her drawer for the take-out menus.

Her phone chimed from its spot on the granite countertop before she decided between Chinese and Italian. She snatched it from its spot, staring down at the message from her aging father. She dismissed the notification before she even read the entire message.

Just because she'd inherit his fortune didn't mean he owned her. Besides, she wouldn't need it. She was making her own waves in the technology sector. She hardly needed Culpepper Enterprises to round out her fortune. Still, she wouldn't say no when the time came.

But for now, she had other pressing matters to attend to. She placed an order for Sweet and Sour Chicken before she wandered to the desk across her loft-style New York City penthouse apartment.

The note—the one that had caused her enough consternation to burn her stir fry—still laid on the dark wood.

The black type contrasted starkly with the white paper. Typed on an old-fashioned typewriter, it chilled her to the bone.

Dear Ms. Kelly Culpepper,

Congratulations on your recent success in the business world. Your ambition has not gone unnoticed.

I invite you to join me for an exclusive gathering on my private island. It will be an opportunity to discuss mutual interests.

Come prepared to confront your past and embrace the future. Your presence is expected, and your compliance is non-negotiable. Failure to meet my demand will result in a less than satisfying conclusion for you.

Yours truly,
Alexander Drake

Instructions for arriving followed. Kelly pressed her lips

together, staving off another shiver as she read the note again. It wasn't just the sinister words typed so neatly on the page, but the name at the bottom. *Alexander Drake.* A man whom she'd faced off with in business…and cheated out of a company.

Exposure of that small detail could ruin her. But a trip to his private island could prove just as disastrous.

II - HEATHER

Heather's fingers worked briskly as she intertwined thread with her knitting needles, weaving together the fabric into a new creation. The repetitive motion, usually a soothing comfort, failed to distract her troubled mind.

She stared down at the red yarn, wrinkling her nose. It suddenly reminded her too much of blood. With a deep sigh, she shoved the work away from her, opting to escape her third-floor walk-up for a stroll through the nearby park.

She left her apartment behind, but her thoughts remained tethered there, stuck on the invitation she'd received earlier. Not even the music floating into her ears could distract her.

The late afternoon sun warmed her skin as she passed from under the shade of a large maple tree. Her phone's display lit with a text.

She chewed her lower lip as she read the message from her younger son. *Going away? Really?*

She heaved a sigh, the question stopping her in her tracks. Her trembling fingers hovered over the virtual keyboard as she tried to formulate a response. *Just for the weekend.*

With the phone shoved in her pocket, she continued along the cobblestone path. The slight breeze, though warm, sent a shiver snaking down her spine. The trip may be just for the weekend, but what would come of it remained a mystery. And something she did not want to face.

The idea soured her walk, and she returned to her apartment, hurrying to push inside before anyone caught her to talk. She didn't want to talk.

She didn't like talking to others on a good day, but on a bad one it seemed ten times worse.

As she stepped inside the safety of her apartment, her eyes fell on to the invitation. The stark black typed letters stood out against the white page.

She picked up the note, her lips tugging into a deep frown as she read the words again.

Dear Ms. Heather Baker,

Congratulations on your recent sales from your art gallery. Your ambition has not gone unnoticed.

I invite you to join me for an exclusive gathering on my private island. It will be an opportunity to discuss mutual interests.

Come prepared to confront your past and embrace the future. Your presence is expected, and your compliance is non-negotiable. Failure to meet my demand will result in a less than satisfying conclusion for you.

Yours truly,
Alexander Drake

She perused the instructions for arriving, shifting her weight from foot to foot as her stomach twisted into a tight knot. The eerie words about her past and her future shook her to the core, but not more than the name on the invitation. Alexander Drake had a bit of knowledge he shouldn't. And it threatened to ruin her life.

III - DAWN

Dawn pushed a blonde lock of hair over her shoulder before she pinched a stray strand from the soft fabric of her designer suit. She glanced down at the book in her lap, unable to concentrate on her favorite pastime while in the air.

With a sigh, she snapped the novel shut and tossed it to the side. Her latest trip had been successful. That was until the arrival of the ominous note.

The contents were one thing, but the fact that it had been delivered to her Paris hotel had been another matter entirely. The man who had sent it was apparently keeping tabs on her.

The idea twisted her stomach into a tight knot. As a politician, she was used to scrutiny. But the scrutiny the note hinted at wasn't the sort that won elections. It was the kind that destroyed careers.

She shifted in her seat, staring out over the bright blue sky dotted with white clouds. Her nose wrinkled at it. How dare the sky be so sunny when her mood was anything but.

The flight attendant approached her first-class seat with a fake smile plastered across her features. "Is there anything I can get you, Senator?"

A new life, Dawn thought, but instead offered the woman a practiced smile as she shook her head. "Another Bloody Mary."

"Of course."

She pulled her book open again, determined to allow the words to soothe her, but she found reading impossible. Instead, she abandoned her favorite pastime in favor of a long sip of the freshly delivered drink and a bite into the celery stalk that accompanied it.

As she chewed the crunchy vegetable, her mind flitted back to the cryptic message. She set her glass aside and fished her bag from under the seat in front of her. With a quick, sly glance around at the other passengers, she slipped the note from the leather briefcase.

Her heart thudded as she opened it up, noting the crisp black letters on the white sheet.

Dear Senator Dawn Angel,

Congratulations on the recent passing of your sponsored bill. Your ambition has not gone unnoticed.

I invite you to join me for an exclusive gathering on my private island. It will be an opportunity to discuss mutual interests.

Come prepared to confront your past and embrace the future. Your presence is expected, and your compliance is non-negotiable. Failure to meet my demand will result in a less than satisfying conclusion for you.

Yours truly,

Alexander Drake

The instructions for her arrival had prompted her to cut her trip to France short. She shifted in the soft leather of the plane's seat, her eyes focusing on the words "sponsored bill." She had a big win in Congress, but it came at a cost. And it appeared that she was now going to pay the price for it.

IV - BONNIE

Bonnie flicked her brush across the canvas, blending a colorful autumn oak tree's leaves into the surrounding sunset. Instead of her usual light touch, though, these brush strokes where hard and forceful, a physical manifestation of the frustration she'd felt since she received her mail this morning.

She leaned back to study her painting, wrinkling her nose

at it before she tossed the brush down and left the easel behind. She collapsed on the chaise in her studio as she stared out at the rainy day.

Droplets of water slid down the windows, reminding her of tears. She flicked her gaze away from the window and tugged her laptop onto her lap.

With her current novel's manuscript open, she stared at the blinking cursor. She couldn't make progress on any front. She'd left the empty page behind in favor of painting. When the painting had gone wrong, she hoped the words would come, but nothing worked.

Nothing would work, either, after she'd received the ominous invitation.

She slammed the laptop shut and shoved it away, a sigh of disgust escaping her. The chime of her phone drew her attention away from her misery. But one quick glance at the display brought it back in spades.

She stared at the message glowing from her screen. *Do you think you'll have the first chapter by next week?*

She frowned at her editor's name. First chapter? She'd be lucky to have the first word by next week.

Following up on her bestselling novel hadn't been easy. Especially when she hadn't written her bestseller. She'd stolen it.

Writing a follow-up novel to the critically acclaimed book was impossible.

She buried her head in her hands and slumped forward. Her gaze landed on the envelope that had caused so much consternation earlier.

She snatched it from the floor next to her chaise and pulled the note out, focusing on the neatly typed letters.

Dear Bonnie Marchitto,

Congratulations on your recent bestseller. Your ambition has not gone unnoticed.

I invite you to join me for an exclusive gathering on my private island. It will be an opportunity to discuss mutual interests.

Come prepared to confront your past and embrace the future. Your presence is expected, and your compliance is non-negotiable. Failure to meet my demand will result in a less than satisfying conclusion for you.

Yours truly,

Alexander Drake

Her nose wrinkled at the instructions that followed on the summons. She didn't want to attend, but she had no choice. She would have to go. And hope it wasn't her undoing.

V - JOANN

Joann sat back on her heels and wiped at a bead of sweat as she grimaced at the turned-up dirt in front of her. She meant to weed her garden, not destroy it. She got a little overzealous as her worried mind pressed her thoughts to dwell on the invitation she'd received earlier in the mail.

Her careless fingers had then tugged away too many things from the soil, resulting in a mishmash of broken flowers and leafless plants. She stared down at the pile of withering greens next to her, tugging off her gloves.

She grabbed the handles of the grocery bag she'd filled and climbed to her feet. After dumping the trash in the bin near the back door, she pushed into the quiet coolness of the house. A cat dashed past her, racing into the living room to leap onto her favorite chair.

"I'm coming, Moxie," she said with a sigh. "As soon as I get out of these dirty clothes."

The destruction of her garden hadn't managed to loosen any of the worry clinging to her, but maybe one of her favorite crime shows would.

She peeled off her gardening gear and replaced it with something more comfortable before she settled into the recliner in front of the television. Moxie leapt onto her lap and curled into a ball while her second cat, Ginger, took a spot on the back of the chair.

As the British mystery series droned on in the background, she found her mind wandering back to the ominous note. Her nose wrinkled at the sender. Her former business partner. And a name she'd never hoped to hear again.

After their falling out over what he claimed was embezzlement, she wanted nothing more than to part ways and never deal with the man again, but that would not be the case.

Her eyes fell to the envelope on her side table. Instinctively, she reached for it and pulled the letter from inside.

Dear Joann Emmons,

Congratulations on your financial upturn. Your ambition has not gone unnoticed.

I invite you to join me for an exclusive gathering on my private island. It will be an opportunity to discuss mutual interests.

Come prepared to confront your past and embrace the future. Your presence is expected, and your compliance is non-negotiable. Failure to meet my demand will result in a less than satisfying conclusion for you.

Yours truly,

Alexander Drake

"Financial upturn," she said with a scoff. "What a joke."

But no matter her thoughts on the matter, she'd have to attend his soiree. Even if it would land her in hot water.

VI - EDWARD

Edward flicked his brush across the paper, a splay of pastel pink coloring what he hoped would be a sunrise scene on his latest watercolor. But the beauty he attempted to create was marred by the black mark hanging over his life.

After cleaning it, he smeared the brush into a light blue shade and streaked it across the picture before he frowned. It was no use. He couldn't concentrate on the painting.

He tossed the brush in the water container and set the paints down before he rose and crossed to the window.

With his hands shoved into his pockets, he stared out at the rainy day. It matched his dreary mood.

He wandered away and plopped into his favorite chair, pulling the newspaper closer. A quick look at the financial section gave him no additional information about the latest trends in the market than it had fifteen minutes ago.

He tossed it aside in favor of a program on the history station about the American Revolution. Although a favorite subject of his, even that couldn't hold his interest.

Instead, his thoughts continued to drift back to the invitation he'd received earlier. A shiver ran down his spine as the words floated across his mind. He frowned, pushing himself up from the comfort of his chair and navigating to the foyer table where he'd tossed it earlier.

He grabbed the envelope and pulled the letter out, his forehead creasing as he read the words again.

Dear Edward Douglas,

Congratulations on your recent success in the stock market. Your ambition has not gone unnoticed.

I invite you to join me for an exclusive gathering on my private island. It will be an opportunity to discuss mutual interests.

Come prepared to confront your past and embrace the future. Your presence is expected, and your compliance is non-negotiable. Failure to meet my demand will result in a less than satisfying conclusion for you.

Yours truly,

Alexander Drake

The information that followed read as a set of demands rather than information for attendance. But the subtle reference to the stock market made him shudder. Alexander Drake knew too much about what had happened when he'd been president of the Mayberry Savings and Trust. And he couldn't afford to have any of it come to light.

VII - PAM

Pam peered at herself in the mirror, ruffling her blonde hair with her fingers before she finished drying her hands with the paper towel. She pitched it away before she adjusted her glasses on her nose again.

She should have worn her contacts today, but she'd slept through her first alarm. She normally never did that, but the lack of sleep she'd gotten the night before left her exhausted.

She pushed out of the ladies' room, heading back to the lab for another round of work. She'd be lucky to stay awake through it. Or be able to concentrate.

The note she'd received yesterday, the one that had rattled her to her core, had been the culprit for her sleepless night and this lack of focus.

She adjusted her glasses again, using the action to try to avoid a conversation with a coworker who passed her in the hall. She normally loved speaking with her colleagues, discussing experiments, posing questions, but today...today she didn't love anything.

Today, her cheerful, spunky nature had been popped and now lay in a puddle on the floor like a melted ice cube.

She pushed into the lab and collapsed on a stool in front of the microscope. With determination, she slid a slide onto the stage and peered through the eyepieces. She turned the knob to bring the cells into focus, studying them before she jotted down her notes.

She took a second look, then tried to detail her observations, but froze mid-word. Her mind blanked, and she couldn't come up with the word she wanted to use to describe the cellular structure.

With a fist gently tapping her forehead, she tried to search the corners of her mind, but the word wouldn't come. All she could focus on was the note she'd received.

She shoved the notebook aside and leaned over to dig into her bag, pulling the envelope from it. After a glance around to ensure she was alone, she slid the paper from inside and read the note again.

Dear Pam Keller Scott,

Congratulations on the success of your recent scientific experiments. Your ambition has not gone unnoticed.

I invite you to join me for an exclusive gathering on my private island. It will be an opportunity to discuss mutual interests.

Come prepared to confront your past and embrace the future. Your presence is expected, and your compliance is non-negotiable. Failure to meet my demand will result in a less than satisfying conclusion for you.

Yours truly,
Alexander Drake

Her features pinched as she stared at the demand. She had no choice but to obey. She only hoped she would come back unscathed.

VIII - DENISE

Denise flicked the page on her latest mystery novel before she lifted her eyes to the lake's calm waters. Despite being an avid reader, she couldn't focus on the words on the page today.

Reading and crafting had been her solace after the incident that ruined her career as a distinguished surgeon. One kept her mind sharp, and the other kept her hands moving.

Usually, one of those tasks could distract her mind. In fact, they'd done such a good job of it that she just started coming out of the funk she plunged into since she resigned her position at the hospital.

But today, neither could do any good. And she felt herself slipping into the morose that had filled her days after she'd left St. Mary's behind.

Her nose wrinkled as she tossed the book aside. Just as she'd been making strides, that ominous note had arrived and sent her into a tailspin.

She'd spent a day in denial, refusing to believe it and desperately trying to convince herself that she could avoid the situation entirely.

Though the note had been more than clear. She sucked in a breath of the fresh mountain air before she tossed the book aside and stretched in her chair.

Her phone chimed, and she checked it, finding a message from her teenage granddaughter. Not even it could lift her spirits. She forced her fingers to type out an answer before she returned to her moody contemplation.

After a few moments, she gathered her book and left her Adirondack chair behind. The water provided few soothing qualities today. As she pushed into the cabin, the scent of wood polish and lavender filled her nostrils. She spotted the enveloped that she'd received yesterday.

She tossed the book on the entryway table and snatched the missive, pulling the paper from the inside.

The black letters so neatly typed against the white page were just as distressing on this read.

Dear Denise Brzezinski,

Congratulations on your recent so-called retirement. Your distinguished career has not gone unnoticed.

I invite you to join me for an exclusive gathering on my private island. It will be an opportunity to discuss mutual interests.

Come prepared to confront your past and embrace the future. Your presence is expected, and your compliance is non-negotiable. Failure to meet my demand will result in a less than satisfying conclusion for you.

Yours truly,
Alexander Drake

Her nose wrinkled at the demand. Her once illustrious career had melted into oblivion when she retired rather than face a formal inquiry into her practices. She thought she had put it behind her, but it seemed her misdeeds had just reared their ugly head. And may prove to ruin her still.

IX - TAMMY

Tammy sat on the bench in the active park, watching the people go by. Her lips tugged into a tight frown as she crossed her arms tightly, her version of shutting herself off from the world.

She didn't mind watching people, but she didn't like talking to them. Unfortunately, it was often part of her job as a journalist, though she preferred deep dives into research to create her stories rather than interviews.

There was a reason she was an introvert. People had a tendency to lie even when they had no reason to.

Whether it was to get quoted in an article, to seem more important than they were, or simply because they had an axe to grind, people lied all the time.

A passerby veered closer to her, sliding on the bench next to her. She sprang up from her seat and moved on.

Today, she was in even less of a mood to deal with people that normal. Her fingers tightened around her purse strap, and before she knew it, she found herself digging inside to retrieve the envelope she hadn't stopped thinking about since it arrived on her desk earlier.

She shoved a strawberry blonde curl aside as she settled onto another bench under a large oak tree. Without wanting to, she pulled the letter from within. Her cheeks puffed out as she read it, her stomach twisting into a knot.

Dear Tammy Shortino,

Congratulations on your recent sensational article. Your distinguished career has not gone unnoticed.

I invite you to join me for an exclusive gathering on my private island. It will be an opportunity to discuss mutual interests.

Come prepared to confront your past and embrace the future.

Your presence is expected, and your compliance is non-negotiable. Failure to meet my demand will result in a less than satisfying conclusion for you.

Yours truly,
Alexander Drake

The word sensational stuck out to her, a definite dig at the story that had gone viral after she published it. She took heat over it, though she stood by her article. She had to. But now, someone threatened to expose everything. And she hoped it didn't cost her.

X - REGINA

Regina scratched the head of her tiny teacup yorkie before adjusting the bow in the dog's hair. She'd curled up with her furry friend and her latest mystery novel on the dreary after-noon, but her mind couldn't focus.

Not even the task of scouring the page for a typo could keep her intrigued in the book. She tossed the paperback aside and leaned over the side of the chaise to find new reading material. Her fingers landed on the latest script that had been delivered for her perusal.

She snatched it and flopped it open, her nose wrinkling a little. They indicated she'd play the role of Beverly. Beverly was the mother character. She wasn't *that* old. Funny how Hollywood had thirty-year-olds playing teens and forty-year-olds playing their mothers these days.

Annoyance crept over her, adding to the tension she already felt. After a few lines, she pitched the script away. Not only was she still young enough to play the main charac-ter, but she also had another issue weighing on her that stopped her from concentrating on anything.

She ruffled the fur on her darling dog's head as the note

she'd received crept into her mind. Arriving in a plain white envelope, the letter hadn't been very intriguing. It certainly wasn't an invitation to a glitzy party, though those had been few and far between these days. And that wasn't because of her age.

Another incident had occurred that cleaved away many of her so-called friendships. She thought she'd effectively dodged the bullet, but then that note arrived.

She glanced to the side table where it still sat, neatly folded on top of the envelope.

Before she could think better of it, her fingers pulled it toward her and flicked it open.

Dear Regina Kurtz,

Congratulations on your recent roles in Hollywood. Your vigor in gaining them has not gone unnoticed.

I invite you to join me for an exclusive gathering on my private island. It will be an opportunity to discuss mutual interests.

Come prepared to confront your past and embrace the future. Your presence is expected, and your compliance is non-negotiable. Failure to meet my demand will result in a less than satisfying conclusion for you.

Yours truly,

Alexander Drake

She didn't like being summoned. But she didn't have much of a choice. If she wanted to continue being one of the most sought-after actresses in the world, she'd have to attend. And hope it wasn't the end of her career.

CHAPTER 1

$\mathcal{I}$ milled around on the dock, my red sneaker playing with a piece of wood poking up from one of the boards. I shoved my hands into my oversized trench coat, drawing it tighter around me as the damp fog continued to roll in.

My gaze finally raised to the choppy waters that separated me from my destination. *Stormy Island.* I rolled my eyes at the name, though at the moment it seemed fitting.

I pictured a dark cloud hanging over top of it while thunder and lightning bombarded the distant island. It was to be my destination for the weekend. Why, I still wasn't certain.

My fingers found the edge of the note I'd received at my fledgling detective agency the day before last. I dug it out and unfurled it. The paper, limp from the damp air and my constant toying with it, flopped over in my hands as I, once again, read the information.

Dear Charlotte "Charlie" Reed,

Congratulations on opening your new detective agency. Your ambition has not gone unnoticed.

If you would like to start what I am certain will be your illustrious career with a bang, I invite you to my island this weekend for a house party. It is certain to be an illuminating time and a life-changing experience.

Bring formal wear for dinners and a weapon. I am certain you will need it. The weapon, that is, though you will need the formal wear, too.

Yours truly,

Alexander Drake

Instructions for arrival followed the note along with a prepaid retainer for seven times the rate I normally charged. I folded it and glanced around the area again. If there was to be a house party, I would have expected other guests. Had they already been shuttled to the island?

I wasn't late. Yet no boat sat tied to the dock, and no other guests stood with me.

I shoved the paper back into my pocket and wondered if I had been had.

The first thing I did after receiving the note had been to research Mr. Alexander Drake. The fellow turned out to be rather an odd duck: a reclusive billionaire who had purchased the island not long ago for pennies on the dollar.

Apparently, Stormy Island wasn't the seaside getaway celebrities and rich folks clamored for. It had a nasty reputation and even nastier weather.

I puckered my lips as my gaze fell on the house perched on top of it. What was Mr. Alexander Drake up to?

My research hadn't turned up much else. Apparently, Mr. Drake had a number of connections but hadn't been seen in many years.

I shoved my hands in my pockets again to warm them.

The check hadn't bounced, so I supposed I owed it to him to stand in the dampness a little longer.

My hair would never recover from it, though. I passed the time trying to vet ways to revive my limp waves for the formal dinner, though I knew it would be a losing battle.

Before I could give it any more thought, a black car pulled up to the dock. The woman inside tossed some bills at the driver before she emerged from the back. My eyebrow arched as I recognized Regina Kurtz, the renowned actress. She was as glamorous as ever, with her perfectly styled blonde hair pulled into an updo, not a strand out of place despite the damp air. Her emerald green eyes scanned the dock with the practiced aloofness of a woman used to adoration.

My heart rose in my throat as, after retrieving her wheeled luggage from the driver, she thumped it along the planks toward me. "Where's the boat?" she asked me.

"Uhhh, I don't know," I answered with a shrug, trying desperately to tuck a lock of my frizzy red hair behind my ear.

Regina set her gaze out across the ocean, her hair and makeup flawless, making me even more self-conscious. "What are you doing here then?"

"Going to Stormy Island?" I said, my voice more of a question than a statement.

She glanced at me, her eyes going up and down my form before she clicked her tongue. "You don't say."

Two more cars made their way to the dock, dropping off two people I didn't know. One was a taller woman with curly, coppery hair blowing in the gentle breeze. The other, in contrast, was petite, with strawberry blonde hair framing her round face.

I wondered if this would be a group of just ladies as three more women arrived.

Within minutes, ten of us stood on the dock, all women. I wondered if everyone was a mistress of our intrepid host. I wasn't, but I wondered if the others were.

Then a lone man showed up. Was he our host? I narrowed my eyes at him. He didn't look like a reclusive billionaire. And I figured the host wouldn't take the boat over with us peons.

Just as I was about to propose that we introduce ourselves, the sound of an engine cut through the growing fog.

My heart rose in my throat for some unbeknownst reason. I was starting off to be a really poor investigator if I was terrified to head to an island with ten strangers for what would be "life changing."

I chewed my lower lip as the small boat finally emerged from the fog wall and pulled closer to the docks.

A man in a fraying jacket and a plaid cap leapt from the boat with a rope in hand, tying off the boat. "You folks ready?"

"No," Regina shouted.

"I'm with Regina," another woman said before several others agreed, chiming in with similar statements.

"Look, maybe if you explained more to us about what we're all doing here," I said.

"Master of the house said to bring the people on the dock to the island. Said if someone didn't want to come, I was to remind them…"

He stopped speaking as he dug into his pocket and pulled out a paper. After unfurling it, he read in a deliberate voice. "Failure to meet his demand will result in a less than satisfying conclusion for you."

He cleared his throat as he folded the note and shoved it back into his pocket before he raised his eyes to us.

Regina fluttered her long eyelashes and shoved her bag

forward. "Fine. Here is my bag. I expect our luggage will be handled."

"Of course," he said as he shuttled the bag to the boat and helped Regina climb aboard.

The others followed suit, and within a few minutes, everyone was loaded, and we were motoring through the soup.

I pulled my trench coat tighter around me as one of the women, dark-haired with gray highlights, plopped down next to me. "Hi, I'm Joann."

She thrust her hand forward as the boat swayed a little too much for my taste. I gripped it harder than I expected, offering her an apologetic smile. "Charlie."

She glanced around at the others. "So, do you have any idea who all these other people are?"

"Um, well, that's Regina Kutcher. She's a pretty actress."

Joann bobbed her head. "Right. Her I recognize. And that one…" She wiggled a finger at pretty blonde who stared out over the water as we traversed it. "That's Bonnie Marchitto. She's a pretty famous novelist."

"Oh, hmm, I wonder if anyone else is famous. Are you famous?" I asked.

She shook her head. "No. Just a simple businesswoman. How about you?"

"No, I'm a…" I hesitated, suddenly not sure I should reveal that I was a private investigator. "Sorry, seasick," I said to cover my pause. "Uhh, I'm a dog walker."

Her brow furrowed. "Oh. Hmm. Well, sorry you're sick." She patted my arm. "It's not a long trip."

My interest perked up immediately. "You've been here before?"

"A few times, yes. Alexander is an old friend."

I logged the information in my mind as I wondered if the

rest of the group had a personal connection to Alexander Drake.

"Do you know him?" Joanna prodded.

"No, umm, I received a note that said he'd gotten my name from someone as a reference. So, I guess I'll be walking the dog this weekend." I chuckled, tucking a lock of my frizzy red hair back.

Joann laughed too before she tilted her head. "He doesn't have a dog."

I silently cursed the stupidity of my choice to lie about my profession in such a ridiculous way. "Oh, maybe he got a new one and that's why I'm here."

"We'll see," she answered as the engine noise died down to a low growl.

I swallowed hard, searching for the dock, but not finding it. I sure hoped the guy piloting our boat knew where it was. Visions of us plunging into the icy waters as our boat rammed into the rocky coastline haunted my mind.

I clutched the side of the boat until my knuckles turned white. A second later, a wooden dock materialized out of the fog. We slid alongside it, bumping against it softly before the driver leapt to the dock to tie us off.

I swallowed hard as the others shifted toward the dock, making the boat rock precariously. The fog seemed thicker now, almost tangible as it wrapped around us, muffling sound and obscuring vision. My stomach twisted as I thought about what lay ahead. Who was Alexander Drake, really? And what kind of man sends an invitation with such a cryptic, threatening tone?

Joann's voice broke through my thoughts. "We won't tip," she said with a soft smile. I nodded, trying to muster a smile in return, but it felt weak, forced. What kind of detective was I if I couldn't even calm my nerves on a simple boat ride?

As I stepped onto the dock, the wood creaking underfoot,

I hesitated. The island loomed ahead, the dark shape of the house barely visible through the thick fog. It felt like stepping into another world—one where danger lurked behind every shadow.

"Thanks," I answered, rubbing at my temples where a throbbing had started.

The boatman helped several people onto the dock before I finally rose on shaky legs.

For a moment, I wondered if I should sit back down and ask him to take me back to the mainland.

"Coming?" Joann asked, pulling me back from my own thoughts. Some PI I was if I jumped ship—no pun intended— at the first sign of trouble. But the island, shrouded in ominous mist, sent a shiver down my spine.

I swallowed hard as I climbed up onto the wooden boards and tugged at my trench coat.

"I hope there's a shuttle," Regina said, adjusting her wrap around her as she stared at the man.

He shook his head as he started to unload the luggage from the stack at the back of the boat. "Nope. Only have a cart to take the luggage up. You want to ride on that?"

I spotted a rickety metal double decker luggage cart that looked like it wouldn't hold up under the weight of our bags.

"I'll pass," Regina said, clearly unimpressed.

"The walk's not too bad," Joann said, pushing through the crowd as she dragged me behind her. "It's just a little winding."

"Have you been here before?" a tall blonde asked.

"Several times," Joann answered, adjusting her purse strap. "This way."

I climbed up the path behind her, one worn into the rocks around us. As we curved around another switchback, the dark form of the house loomed over us.

I swallowed hard as I stared at the sprawling place, wondering what secrets it held.

Who would bring together a businesswoman, an actress, a novelist, a private investigator, and whoever else these people were?

I swallowed hard when we finally got close enough to make out the details of the large mansion. Gingerbread trim laced the entire outline, but this wasn't the cute white curls of a Victorian. These were black twists that curled like gnarled fingers reaching for my very soul.

Spiked spires clawed at the dark sky as though reaching for release from this world.

The darkened windows looked like they led to a void. And a black door with a grisly lion door knocker stood the center.

When we finally reached the front door, Joann raised her hand to use the knocker, but the door creaked open, its hinges groaning ominously like a warning to run.

Instead, we all ignored it, plowing inside, pleased to be out of the damp weather.

The moment we'd all entered the foyer, thunder boomed overhead, rumbling for several seconds.

The single male in our group pushed the door closed, and the moment it clicked shut, a voice sounded.

We all searched for the source, but it seemed to come from everywhere all at once.

"Welcome treasured guests. I'm so glad you could all make it.

"I do hope you found your trip enjoyable and that you will find your accommodations equally pleasing. Heaven knows, you will need it to be. Because what you are about to experience will leave you drained to say the least.

"You see, each of you is here for a reason. Each of you has

a past. A past filled with something you hoped would never come to light.

"But I have discovered your secrets. And soon you will be faced with a choice. Your secret or your life.

"But for now…enjoy your evening. Room assignments are on the foyer table. Every effort has been made to ensure your comfort.

"Retire to your rooms now and rest before you dress for dinner. Cocktails are at six. Be prompt.

"Your lives depend on it."

A maniacal laugh filled the foyer, echoing off the marble floors and the tall columns holding the high ceiling at bay. I swallowed hard, a chill running down my spine. This wasn't just a weekend retreat. It was a trap—one carefully laid out by a man who seemed to know everything about us. My heart pounded in my chest as the reality of the situation sank in. Our secrets or our lives? What kind of choice was that?

I was supposed to be a detective, someone who could outsmart the bad guys, but right now, I felt like a mouse caught in a cat's game. And the worst part? I didn't even know who the cat was. All I knew was that if I didn't figure this out—and fast—none of us were getting off this island alive.

CHAPTER 2

*J*paced the area rug poking from under the four-poster bed in the suite larger than my apartment. My nerves hadn't settled since the ominous message we'd heard upon our arrival.

Of course, no one said anything after it. Instead, everyone glanced around at each other suspiciously while acting like they had no idea what our illustrious host was talking about.

And maybe they didn't. I bit my thumbnail as I spun on a heel and stalked back in the opposite direction.

I didn't have a secret. At least, not that I knew of. I mean, once I'd cheated on an exam because I couldn't recall the difference between set operators in my college mathematics class. But I'd merely scrawled a note onto my hand just before it and most of it had wiped off before I could use the information anyway because my palms were so sweaty.

Had Alexander Drake somehow known about my college misdeed?

I fluttered my eyelashes, finally leaving my self-imposed prison of the rug behind and wandering to the window. I plopped onto the window seat's thick cushion and grabbed a tasseled throw pillow as I stared out over the landscape.

The mists were moving away, but the sky was darkening, and the sea in the distance had turned far choppier than it had been on our trip in.

I appreciated getting on the boat when I did, because I'd never have made it over in this weather.

I flicked my gaze up at the black clouds that hovered above the island. They didn't seem to be moving, instead simply stuck above us as they churned round and round.

As I stared up, a bolt of lightning lit the inside of the dark cloud before it snaked through the sky.

I flinched, leaning away from the thick glass as the first few raindrops pelted it. Within minutes, it had turned into a steady downpour with thunder rumbling overhead.

The lights flickered a few times, stopping my heart for an instant, before they thrummed back to life.

I blew out a sigh of relief as I went to my suitcase that had arrived mysteriously in my room before I found it and dragged it onto the luggage rack. Unzipping it, I flung it open and dug through for something suitable to wear.

After receiving my advance, I bought a few evening dresses for the occasion, since I'd been told I would need them. They all seemed to pale in comparison to what I expected the others to wear.

Nevertheless, it was all I had, so I grabbed the silky green cocktail dress and a few accessories and headed into my en-suite bathroom to pull myself together.

I emerged forty-five minutes later with my hair just as disheveled as when I'd gone in, but with a fancy, bejeweled clip making a desperate attempt to hold it back.

I slicked on a little makeup, but I wasn't very good at that sort of thing, so I ended up with raccoon eyes instead of smokey ones. I folded up my clothes and nestled them in my suitcase before I pulled my pajamas out for later.

With the storm still raging, I wanted to climb into them now and curl up with a good book.

Instead, I slipped into a pair of heels and wobbled my way down the hall toward the sweeping staircase that led to the foyer below.

I didn't make it halfway when I trudged back to my room and swapped the heels for the red sneakers I'd worn earlier. With the length of the dress, no one would even see them, and I'd be comfortable.

As I emerged from my room a second time, I ran into a brunette. Her sparkling blue eyes smiled at me before her lips did.

"Heading down?" she asked as she gripped her dark blue satin evening bag.

"I am. I'm Charlie, by the way."

"Kelly," she said with a grin. "Do I know you?"

I shook my head as I lifted my skirt, awkwardly flashing my red sneakers. "No, I don't think so."

As we trudged through the dimly lit hallway, I noticed a small door off to the side, partially hidden behind a heavy curtain. It was so out of place, tucked away where no one would normally see it. I made a mental note to check it out later—if I got the chance.

"Oh, I thought I'd seen you around the New York scene. You're not an heiress?"

The question made me laugh out loud, and I covered my mouth with a hand as we reached the top of the stairs. "No, definitely not."

"Oh, hmm. I could have sworn I knew you from the Met or something."

"Not quite," I answered. "Are you an heiress?"

I slid my eyes sideways as she gracefully descended the stairs. "Oh, yes, Culpepper Enterprises."

"Right," I said, immediately recognizing the name. Kelly Culpepper was one of New York's most eligible bachelorettes, though no one could figure why she'd not been snapped up. Did it have something to do with her secret?

I couldn't ask anything more as we arrived in the living room just as the clock struck six. A loud whoosh followed by a smacking noise startled me, and I twisted to find a large blade hanging from the ceiling just outside of the room.

My eyebrows rose as I realized if we'd been a second later, we could have been sliced in half. "Whoa."

"Is that a cleaver?" The lone man charged across the room to look at it.

"He did say be prompt," a blonde with a southern accent said as she stared out at the stormy landscape from a seat by the window.

"And that it meant our lives," the strawberry blonde said.

"Yes, but I didn't know he'd actually try to kill one of us. A bit dramatic, wouldn't you say?" Regina asked.

"You're one to talk," a blonde said as she flicked a lock of her shoulder grazing hair away from her face.

"And just who are you?" Regina asked.

"None of your business," she shot back.

"Okay, ummm, not to be presumptuous, but it seems like we're going to be spending the entire weekend together. I, for one, would like to at least know everyone's names," I said with a shrug.

"Oh, would you, Red?" the aggressive blonde asked. "Why don't you go first then?"

"Okay," I said with a deep breath. "I'm Charlie Reed. I'm a dog walker. And I'm guessing everyone else here, like I did, received a note inviting them to spend the weekend."

Silence stretched in the room, only the rumbles of thunder and pattering of rain on the windows breaking it.

"Well, Charlie," Joann said as she lifted her glass of sherry in the air, "I'm Joann Emmons. I'm an entrepreneur. And I did receive a letter, too."

"What did yours say?" the blonde asked.

"I imagine the same as everyone else's. That I was invited here for the weekend. Now, Charlie and I have played, how about someone else?" Joann searched the others' faces.

"No one else agreed to play," Regina said, a coy expression on her face.

"We all know who you are," the strawberry blonde answered with a roll of her eyes.

Regina smiled to herself, her eyebrows arching. "Well, good. Then everyone knows I'm Regina Kurtz, world famous actress."

I poured a brandy and pretended to sip it. If I wanted to learn anything, I needed to play the game but keep my wits about me.

"Fine," another blonde spoke up. "I'm Bonnie Marchitto—"

"Famous novelist," Joann finished for her.

Bonnie offered her a self-assured smile as she raised her brandy, her straight blonde hair framing her face like a halo. Despite her calm demeanor, there was a sharpness in her eyes that suggested she was always analyzing, always thinking.

"Uh, I'll go next," the sole man among us said. "I'm Edward. I'm a banker."

The curly, copper-haired woman plopped onto the couch with a sigh. "Heather. Art."

The tall blonde near the fireplace stared into her drink. "Dawn. State senator."

"Tammy," the strawberry blonde said as she sauntered to

the window. "Journalist. This weather is really something, huh?"

"The storm's raged for a while now. It doesn't seem to be moving," Edward said.

Kelly introduced herself, telling everyone she was an executive with Culpepper industries.

That left the two blondes, the quieter one, and the more aggressive one. All eyes fell on them. The quieter one rose from her seat. "Fine. I'm Pam. I'm a scientist."

With a sigh, the other one shook her head. "Seriously?"

"Come on," Joann said. "You're the only one who hasn't given your name and occupation."

She offered her a glare. "Denise. Doctor."

I mulled over the list. Nothing seemed to connect any of these people together. They came from all walks of life. But according to our illustrious host, they all had a secret. But what? I could understand if they'd all come from the same company board or state, but they seemed to have nothing in common at all.

"Well," Denise said with a heavy sigh, "that did us a whole lot of good, didn't it?"

"Well," I answered with a shrug, "at least we know each other's names. It would have been a pretty difficult weekend to get through if I had to just nickname you all in my head." I chuckled at the idea.

"What?" Denise asked. "What nickname did you use for me?"

I laughed nervously again. "No, I didn't. That's what I'm saying, though. I didn't use nicknames because now I know your name is Denise."

"But how did you refer to me before in your mind?"

"Blonde woman?" I answered, my voice a question.

"There's a lot of blondes," Pam answered, crossing her arms. "Were we all 'blonde woman'?"

I wrinkled my nose. "Uhhh…"

"Clearly not," Regina said with a sweep of her hand. "I was Regina. Everyone knew me."

"That still leaves how many 'blonde women' left?" Pam set her hands on her hips.

"Look, the point is, now I don't have to do that," I tried to reiterate when another boom of thunder shook the windows in their panes.

The lights flickered before they went out. For a split second, the room was plunged into darkness, and all I could hear was the pounding rain and the quickened breaths of the others. A hand brushed against mine—too quick to be comforting. My heart raced as I imagined what could happen in the dark, surrounded by people I didn't know with secrets I couldn't guess.

Shrieks went up through the room before the lights finally glowed back to life. I quickly counted us up, pleased to see all eleven of us alive. I had sincerely worried that we would end up in some sort of Agatha Christie scenario with people dropping off like flies.

Pam set her glass down with a shake of her head. "That's it. I'm out of here. I'm not going to stay another minute on this creepy island. I'm leaving."

"How?" Joann asked.

"We'll take the boat," Regina said with a raise of her chin. "I'm with you, Pam."

"Who else?" Pam asked as she linked arms with the actress.

A few others agreed, including Kelly, Tammy, and Dawn.

As they headed for the door, the rest of us followed. Regina tugged the front door open. Rain battered the walkway out front, pouring from the skies.

"We'll be soaked," Heather shouted over the din.

"I'd rather be soaked than stay here," Denise said.

"What about our luggage?" Heather asked.

"Leave it. We can send for it later," Bonnie answered. "Let's go!"

Before we could head into the messy weather, a voice boomed behind us. "Stop there!"

I turned to spot the boatman from earlier. "You can't go out there," he added.

"Why not?" Joann asked.

"There's no way off this island," he answered. "Not with the storm. The boat's been smashed against the rocks. And the communication lines are down. You're trapped here."

A sinking feeling filled my stomach as he said the words. We were trapped here. Trapped. My mind raced through the possibilities, none of them good. What kind of game was Alexander Drake playing? And how were we supposed to survive it? I tried to steady my breathing, reminding myself that I was a detective. I was here to figure things out, not to panic. But the truth was, I was terrified.

CHAPTER 3

$\mathcal{A}$s gasps went up among the group, my stomach clenched into a tight knot. It was one thing to be here for the weekend, and quite another to be stuck. Panic roiled inside of me as I tried desperately to squash it down and behave like a rational adult instead of a raving lunatic.

Regina pushed her way to the front, her hands on her hips. "Just what do you mean?

"I mean, there's no way off the island. The boat was smashed in the earlier winds. And we can't call for help."

Eyes widened as murmurs went up through the crowd. "So, what are we supposed to do? We can't just stay here!" Tammy shouted.

"She's right," Denise said. "What happens when we run out of food?"

"Someone will come on Monday," the man explained. "The clean-up crew will realize something is wrong and send someone."

"And we're supposed to do what?" Heather demanded. "Just sit here and wait?"

The man shrugged. "Enjoy your weekend?"

Edward shook his head. "Okay, wait. All we have is his word that the communication lines are down and the boat is smashed."

"You're right," Dawn said with a poke of her finger. "We don't know that he's telling the truth."

Murmurs went up through the group again before Edward spoke, "I'll go look."

"Wait, you could be lying, too!" Kelly said.

"Two people should go," Joann suggested.

"What if they're in on it together?" Bonnie asked.

"We'll all go!" Regina shouted.

A smattering of applause broke out at the suggestion.

"Wait, wait, I'm not sure I want to go out in that," Denise said.

"Why don't we draw straws?" Joann said. "It's fair, and it's really unlikely that two people working together would end up checking."

The members of our party eyed each other before nodding.

"I saw chimney matches in the living room near the fireplace," Pam said. "We'll break those, and we all pick a stick. The two shortest go. Everyone else stays."

With nods of agreement from the group and a shake of the head from the boatman, we shuffled back into the living room. Edward broke six matches unevenly, tossing one piece back into the box before he shuffled the others and held them up in his hand for us to pick.

One by one, we all took our turn picking a stick, carefully hiding it from the others. I picked fifth and ended up with one that seemed long enough to keep me dry, though my curiosity had kicked in, and I was dying to explore—even in the poor weather.

"All right," Edward said as he held the sole stick left. "Let's compare."

We all held our sticks out; some of us measured to compare close lengths until the two shortest pieces had been ferreted out. The two victims were Kelly and Heather.

Kelly groaned as she tossed her stick into the fire. "I'd really rather not go."

"I'll go in your place," I said.

"No, this is exactly what we were trying to prevent!" Denise answered. "Two people working together."

I heaved a sigh and shook my head. "Look, we'll take pictures, a video even. I'll bring proof back."

Grumbles went up through the group before reluctant acquiescence. "Fine, if you bring pictures," Regina said.

"Wait," Bonnie said. "Let's see both of your phones so that we know you don't have pictures already on there to fake this."

With a heavy sigh, I pulled my phone from my purse and handed it over. A few people looked through my camera reel, sufficiently convinced I had no pictures of a smashed boat already on it.

After a check of Heather's device, we were cleared to go. I retrieved my trench coat from my room, and we found a few umbrellas in the stand near the door.

Despite the thunder and lightning, I held my umbrella above my head to keep the soaking rain from drenching me as we made our way down the winding path to the boat launch.

When we finally reached the bottom, I stared into the water as rain pelted the fabric of my umbrella. Now, only pieces of the boat were swirling around in the frothy water near the dock.

"Oh my gosh, he wasn't lying," I said to Heather as we both snapped pictures of the evidence, including a few pieces washed onto the rocky shore.

As we made our return trip up to the house, our feet slipping on the rain-soaked path, my mind spun. Why would they leave the boat there in a storm like that? Surely it had stormed here before.

Heck, the island was known as Stormy Island. Didn't this happen all the time? Why was the boat smashed this time?

I made a mental note to ask the boatman when we got back—after we delivered the bad news. Although the communication thing seemed to be legitimate. No one had cell phone signal from the time we stepped foot onto the island.

We finally reached the front door and pushed inside, shaking off our umbrellas before stowing them. I was still damp to my core, and the bottom of my dress was wet despite me holding it up. I knew I should have changed before I went to look, but I'd been talked out of it since we needed to be ready for dinner.

The others waited for us in the foyer, gathering around us quickly as we doffed out our jackets.

"Well?" Regina demanded.

"The boat's smashed," I said, flashing them pictures.

Heather shared hers too as more gasps went up through the group.

"So, we're stuck!" Pam shouted, her voice rife with panic.

"Looks like it," I answered, though my mind went back to my original question about how this could happen on an island known for its storms.

"And the communication?" Bonnie questioned.

"None of our cell phones are working, even at the docks," Heather reported. "Whether or not they have some sort of radio that can reach the mainline, I don't know. But our communication is completely blocked."

Exclamations of fear and disappointment floated from the group members.

"Well, now what?" Dawn asked.

Behind the group, someone cleared his throat. All eyes turned toward the man in a crisp black tuxedo. "Dinner," he said simply.

"Whoa, just a minute, buddy," Regina said, her voice thick with emotion. "We're not just going to go to dinner."

"But Mr. Drake insists dinner be promptly at eight. I was to send you to the dining room at precisely this moment."

"Mr. Drake," I said. "Our host. Surely, he'll have some answers for us. Maybe we should go."

The others eyed each other before nods started. "All right," Dawn said. "We'll go. But he'd better have answers."

"Wait, wait," Pam said with a shake of her head. "What about the secrets we have? Are we sure we want to interact with Mr. Drake?"

Tammy arched an eyebrow. "What's your secret that you're so afraid of having exposed?"

Pam lifted a shoulder and shook her head. "Nothing. But he thinks we have something. I don't want him spewing his lies about me."

"All right," Kelly said, setting her hand on her hip. "If we all agree it's lies, then we just won't listen to anything he says. Deal?"

A few nods met her request, and some people shuffled toward the dining room.

"No, wait a second," Denise said with a shake of her head. "Pam's right. Even if it's all lies, I don't want some crazy lie spilled about me, because one of you will believe it!"

Regina scoffed. "Just who are you accusing of being that gullible? I've been in Hollywood for *years*. I don't believe whatever I hear."

"*Someone* will," Denise shot back with narrowed eyes.

Regina stepped closer to her, the challenge obvious, before she looked around at the others. "Who is going to believe the lies?"

No one spoke up, and once again, we started to shuffle toward the dining room.

"Wait, I might," Kelly said with a wrinkled nose.

"What?" Heather asked.

Kelly winced, lifting her shoulders in a shrug. "I'm sorry. But…there's always some truth in every rumor, right?"

"Wrong!" Regina said. "In most rumors, there is no truth whatsoever."

Kelly shifted her weight, refusing to meet Regina's gaze. "I mean…a lot of what I heard on the debutante rumor circle was partly true."

Bonnie crossed her arms. "Fine. All right. Kelly is here because she had a torrid affair with not just any man, but the President himself. She ended up pregnant and had to go to another country to take care of it so as not to call attention to it. That's her secret."

"What?" Kelly curled her fingers into fists as she stamped a foot on the floor. "That's insane. I've never even met the President."

Bonnie lifted a shoulder. "Is there no truth in any of that?"

"Absolutely not," Kelly exclaimed.

"Then there you have it. *Now* can you believe something could be a complete fabrication?"

Kelly's features reddened as her face morphed into an unimpressed mask. "All right, fine. Whatever he says is a complete and utter lie."

"We are all agreed, right?" Regina said.

No one answered.

"*Right?*" Regina repeated, her voice tense.

Slow nods met her question.

"Good," she said. "No one will believe a thing he says, and we concentrate on getting information about how we can get off this island."

Finally, the entire group shuffled to the dining room

doors. I stared at the ornate scrollwork carved into the arched doors leading into the space.

Regina pushed to the front of the group and swung the doors open. "All right, Mr. Drake," she demanded as she headed into the room. "We have questions, and we demand answers."

She set her hands on her hips as she stared down the long table at the man in the chair at the head.

"Yeah," Bonnie added. "You dragged all of us here for no reason, and now we're trapped. What are you doing to make sure we can get home?"

I stepped around them, my eyebrows knitting as I stared down the table. Even at this distance, something seemed off. "Mr. Drake?"

"Don't be so tentative," Joann said. "We want answers, Alexander. Now!"

"Something's wrong," I answered, my breath hitching in my throat.

"You are darn right it is," Heather said with a scoff.

I shook my head. "No. No, I mean, something's wrong with him."

I inched my way forward toward the end of the table, each step feeling like it took an eternity. The air was thick with anticipation, the silence only broken by the distant rumble of thunder.

My heart pounded in my ears as I reached out with trembling fingers, hesitating for just a second before finally touching his sleeve. The fabric felt cold, lifeless. And then he slumped forward, revealing the gruesome truth: the knife buried deep in his back.

Screams erupted from the other guests as we all stared at our host: dead as a doornail. Bonnie clutched her chest, eyes wide with terror, while Regina stumbled back, her composure cracking for the first time. Edward's face drained of color as he muttered something under his breath. I could see the gears turning in their minds—was it shock, or were they already calculating their next move?

My heart hammered as I stared at the knife sticking out of his back, my mind racing through the implications. Whoever had done this had to be among us. Was it one of the people standing right beside me? I had to stay calm, keep my wits about me. This was no longer just a strange weekend getaway—this was a murder investigation, and I was in the middle of it.

CHAPTER 4

I swallowed hard, grabbing the back of a chair to support my wobbling legs. I wanted to be a private investigator, but I never thought that would mean I'd stumble upon a dead body and be stuck on an island with the killer hiding in plain sight.

At least, I assumed one of the other ten had killed him.

I glanced at them over my shoulder, trying to read their expressions. Was someone feigning shock? Which one of them was it? I couldn't tell. I didn't know any of them well enough to know who could be faking that look of sheer surprise.

"We need to call someone!" Kelly exclaimed, her voice shrill with panic—but was it real or fake?

"Who?" I asked. "There is no communication the butler said."

"Well, we can't just leave him here dead on the table," Joann said.

I licked my lips as Edward stepped forward to move him. "Wait, wait…"

"What?" he asked.

"Well, this is a crime scene. We can't move the body. We can't touch anything."

Denise huffed out laugh. "So, we're supposed to leave him slumped over the table with a knife in his back for the entire weekend? Are we supposed to eat our meals in here with the body, too?"

"No, I—"

"Then what?" Heather snapped.

"Okay, let's just all calm down," I said, forcing strength into my voice. "We need to do this methodically."

"Methodically? What are you getting at?" Regina asked.

"I'm getting at the fact that he's dead. Murdered, obviously. Someone here did it. So, we need to preserve whatever evidence we can."

"And just who are you accusing?" Pam shouted at me.

"No one!" I said, my voice strained. "But we need to do things by the book."

Bonnie heaved a sigh. "And I suppose the dog walker knows procedure."

"I…may not be a dog walker," I answered with a wince.

"Are you a cop?" Denise shot back.

"No. I'm a private investigator, though. And I know we need to preserve this crime scene as much as possible."

"So, what do we do?" Kelly asked.

"Well, first, we should make sure he's actually dead."

Scoffs went up from the group as I made the suggestion.

"Seriously?" Denise asked. "He's got a knife sticking out of his back. He's dead, honey."

"Well," I said with a grimace as I inched closer and pressed two fingers to his already-cold skin. I felt no pulse. "Yep, he's dead. Okay, umm, and he's cold, so he didn't just die."

"So, we've been in this house with a dead guy for how long?" Heather asked, her voice shaky.

"I don't know," I admitted. "But this must have happened a few hours ago. Before everyone came down for cocktails."

"Someone else sneaked down here and killed our host," Kelly said.

"But what was he doing at the table?" Dawn asked.

"Maybe someone killed him and moved him," Regina said.

I poked a finger at her. "It could be. There's no blood here."

"Clue number one," Bonnie said as she stepped forward, narrowing her eyes at the victim. "We should search the house for blood to see where he was murdered."

"No, no," Pam said with a shake of her head. "No, we're not splitting up so whichever one of you murdered him can take the rest of us out one by one."

"No one's going to do that," Dawn retorted.

"Why are you assuming one of us is the murderer?" Joann asked. "This house is crawling with staff. Any one of them could have murdered him."

"Oh, dear," the butler said as he stepped into the room with two maids, carrying trays with the first course on it.

"Which one of you did it, huh?" Regina asked, her voice turning into something close to a 1940s gumshoe. "Fess up now before this gets worse for you."

I wrinkled my nose at the over-acted scene. The maids scurried from the room, and the butler set his tray down on the server before he crossed to take Alexander Drake's pulse.

"He's dead. I checked," I told him as he pulled his fingers away with a grimace.

"And maybe one of the staff did it!" Denise said. "We want to see all of you for questioning."

"Impossible, madam," the butler answered. "The staff was not permitted in the house prior to half an hour before the dinner call. Mr. Drake has clearly been dead for several hours."

Regina poked a finger at him. "And how would you know that if you didn't kill him?"

"He's cool to the touch. That means he's been dead for at least two hours. Haven't you ever watched a true crime show?" The man arched an eyebrow high.

"Clearly, we all haven't," I answered, "but that makes sense. So, he was killed before the cocktail hour, just as I said."

"Oh, just as *you* said," Tammy chimed in. "Maybe you did it then."

I heaved a sigh and shook my head. "I didn't do this."

"Well, you did lie to us once already."

"Fine," I said with a lift of my chin. "Search my room if you think I did it. You'll see that there is no evidence there."

"Because you hid it!" Bonnie said with a poke of her finger.

"I did not."

Heather crossed her arms. "We'll never know."

"I'd wager it was one of you," I answered. "You all came to this island with a secret according to our host. And I'd bet one of you killed him to keep it quiet."

"Wow," Regina shot back, crossing her arms as she arched an eyebrow at me. "The mouse roars."

"Yeah, I'm getting a little suspicious of the mouse," Pam said, wagging a finger at me. "You're pointing the finger at everyone. And you're probably the guilty party."

"That's not true."

"No, it's not her," Bonnie said.

Dawn huffed out a sharp laugh. "How do you know?"

"Because I'm a writer. I've written a dozen mysteries. Everyone knows it's not the person you most suspect."

"Oh, I'm so glad to know your mystery writing qualifies you to tell us who is and isn't guilty," Denise said, crossing her arms.

"Yeah," Pam joined in, "so Madam Writer…who *is* guilty?"

"That I don't know. I don't pretend to know everything happening here. I'm just using common sense," Bonnie shot back.

"That's about all you've got," Edward said from the back of the group.

All eyes turned to him as lightning lit the sky and thunder boomed.

"What's that supposed to mean?" Tammy asked.

"It means…we all do have a secret here. And I know Bonnie's."

Bonnie's jaw dropped open as she stared at him before she quickly collected herself. "I don't know what you're talking about, but I would suggest you keep your mouth shut before I sue you."

"You can only sue if it's false," Edward shot back.

"What's the secret?" Joann asked.

"What's your secret?" Bonnie retorted, her hands falling to her hips.

"I don't have one, but it seems you do."

"Stop it!" I shouted, bringing the conversation to a screeching halt. "All right, I think we owe it to everyone to hear what Edward has to say, and then let Bonnie defend herself."

"What?" Bonnie cried, her fingers curling into fists. "This isn't a court of law. I don't have to defend myself."

"Okay, then don't," Pam said. "But Edward has the right to tell us what he knows."

"What he thinks he knows," Joann corrected. "He could be lying."

"Or he could be telling the truth," Denise said.

"Or part of it," Kelly added.

Tammy scoffed, her eyes glassy as she stared at the body.

"Do we really have to do this with a dead body right next to us?"

"Tammy's right," I said with a shake of my head. "We should leave the crime scene behind and lock this door. No one in or out of here until we figure this out."

"We'll set up in the living room. I think we could all use a drink," Regina said, wrapping her arms around Heather and guiding her toward the door.

I stayed back as the others began shuffling out, a few of them glancing over their shoulders at the body before they disappeared into the hall.

I left the room last, closing the doors behind us and telling the butler to lock them. After watching him do it, I made my way to the sitting room, where everyone had settled somewhere with a drink.

I swallowed hard, trying to push down the rising panic. I was supposed to be the calm, collected investigator, but here I was, on the verge of losing it. How did I end up the one calling the shots? This was supposed to be a simple weekend —maybe an odd one, sure—but not a murder mystery with real stakes. And yet, they were all looking to me for answers, for direction. I couldn't let them see how uncertain I was. I needed to be strong, or we'd all fall apart.

I poured myself a brandy as Bonnie paced the room. Edward stood by the fireplace, staring into it.

Heather, Denise, and Kelly huddled on the couch, staring into their drinks.

Joann settled into an armchair, Regina peered out the window, while Dawn and Tammy sat on the piano bench.

"Where's Pam?" I asked, glancing around the room.

"Ladies'," Regina said. "She'll be right back."

I frowned, wondering if she'd gone to remove some evidence or collect herself after seeing the body. No one else seemed to be acting suspiciously, so Pam would be my first suspect.

She finally entered the room, fiddling with her hands as though they were still wet. I wondered if it was a pretense or if she'd actually washed her hands. And had it been because she'd used the restroom or because she was attempting to wash away some evidence?

She settled into a seat after pouring herself a drink.

"All right," Joann said, "let's proceed."

"If we must," Bonnie said, "but this is awful behavior from all of you."

"Noted," Pam answered, "Edward, what do you know?"

"Earlier, Bonnie claimed to be a mystery writer, acting like she knew how to use deductive reasoning to suss out a suspect and determine the killer. But that's not true."

I furrowed my brow as Joann tilted her head. "Of course it is. I recognized her right away."

"You recognized her as a famous author. You got half of that right," Edward answered. "She's famous all right. But she's not an author."

"That's insane," Bonnie shot back as the others offered him puzzled looks.

"What do you mean?" Kelly asked.

The room fell into a tense silence, all eyes fixed on Edward as he prepared to drop his bombshell. I could feel the weight of his words hanging in the air, thick with anticipation. When he finally spoke, his voice was low, almost conspiratorial. "She's famous for writing all those mystery novels, but she didn't write them…she stole them."

My eyes went wide, and I shot a glance at Bonnie to assess her reaction. Had she plagiarized her bestselling novel? And could that have led her to murder?

CHAPTER 5

The silence in the room stretched as people stared at Bonnie, waiting for a response. My stomach clenched, and I held my breath as I wondered if she'd respond, denying it or maybe admitting to it.

Joann shifted in her seat. "Is that true?"

"Of course not," Bonnie said with a shake of her head.

"It is true. Ask her who her current publisher is?" Edward shot back.

Pam flicked a lock of blonde hair from her face. "Who's your publisher?"

Bonnie scoffed. "You're not seriously falling for this cheap trick, are you? He's just trying to deflect the attention away from him. Remember, we *all* have a secret here. Not just me. So instead of asking who my publisher is, maybe we should be focusing on what Edward's big secret is."

"I think we should focus on your secret and whether or not you murdered someone over it," Tammy answered.

"Yeah," Pam answered. "Let's rule people out one by one."

Bonnie heaved a sigh as she shook her head. "How in the world would me answering any questions tell you about my guilt? I mean, I'm not admitting to anything, but even if I did plagiarize it…would I kill over it? No."

"Where were you before the cocktail hour?" I asked.

She narrowed her eyes at me, her hands falling to her hips. "In my room."

"Can anyone verify that?"

"Yes, the small part of people I had gathered in there for my alibi can confirm it," Bonnie shot back.

"We don't need her to confirm her part of the story," Edward said. "I have the emails terminating her from her publisher over the allegations. If they thought it was real, I'd say it is."

Kelly hurried to his side, glancing at his phone before she gasped. "It says here they had some sort of proof."

"What's the proof?" Regina asked, lifting her chin.

"It doesn't say," Kelly said with a shake of her head. "But it says they have enough proof to terminate their contract with her for five additional books."

Bonnie collapsed into an armchair, her fingers digging into the fabric. "How did you get that?"

"Friend of a friend," Edward answered as he stowed his phone. "I know a lot of people, including the president of your publishing company. He passed it along, worried about how it may affect his stock prices. I assured him it would never see the light of day, but given our current circumstances, I thought it should be brought to light because it speaks directly to motive."

"Motive?" Bonnie cried. "You can't be serious."

"I can be. If that got out, you'd be ruined. No one would ever publish you again or read your books. So, you killed Mr. Drake to make sure it didn't."

"That's not true!" she shouted.

"Okay, okay, wait…who has a room near Bonnie's?" I asked as I tried to sort through the logic.

Thunder rumbled overhead as a few people's hands poked in the air. "I spotted Regina, Kelly, and Denise," someone said.

"Did any of you hear anything? Maybe her door opening, maybe footsteps?" I asked.

All of them shook their head.

"Did anyone hear anything?" Denise asked. "That's a good place to start."

People glanced around at each other, but no one mentioned anything.

"If you were going to kill someone, do you really think you'd slam your door and pound your way down the hall?" Edward asked.

I shook my head, trying to parse through the few clues we had. "All right, maybe we should continue on with the secret track."

No one spoke.

"I'm not the only one here with a secret. And mine isn't even that bad," Bonnie said. "I didn't plagiarize. Yes, they have 'evidence' because someone accused me. But I didn't do it. She helped me work out a few passages, then claimed she wrote the book. All of that work is mine."

"According to you. Not according to her," Edward said with a raise of his eyebrows.

"Whatever. I didn't kill anyone over it. And in fact, I've penned my next two novels and soon will be penning a third. And do you know what it'll be about? It'll be a murder mystery with a group of people who get stuck on an island, and the mouthy man bites it."

"And there's the threat," Edward said, poking a finger at her. "Are we really supposed to believe this isn't the face of a killer?"

"Yes, because I only kill people on paper."

"Okay, I'm not sure we can rule anyone out just yet, but as

Bonnie pointed out, she's not the only one who has a secret here," I said, trying to force information out of someone.

"Ohhh, she's right," Heather answered, shifting a lock of her auburn hair. "There's someone else here with a big secret."

People gasped, glancing around to eye each other suspiciously.

"Sounds like you know something," Kelly answered, shifting her weight.

Heather shrugged. "Maybe."

"Now's not really the time to be coy," I answered, my frustration building.

Bonnie rose, her fingers curling into fists. "Yes. I've been accused of killing someone over a spat between authors. So, if someone else is harboring a secret—particularly one that could provide a motive, I'd like to hear it."

"Oh, it would provide a motive all right. And I'm happy to tell what I know, but I thought perhaps the guilty party would like to explain themselves before accusations are made and fingers are pointed."

I studied the others in the room, searching their faces for some guilt or recognition, but everyone wore a similar expression: non-committal, refusing to make eye contact with anyone else in the room.

"Fine," Joann finally said. "I have a secret."

Silence pervaded the space as we all waited for her to speak again.

Joann's fingers tapped nervously against her glass, a slight tremor betraying the calm facade she was trying to maintain. "Alexander Drake and I knew each other personally," she finally admitted, her voice steady but with an edge that hinted at deeper emotions. Was it guilt? Fear? Or something else?

"That's your secret?" Kelly asked with a scoff.

"Well, I'm guessing no one else knew him," Joann answered with a flick of her hair over her shoulder.

No one admitted to anything, but I wasn't surprised. I didn't expect anyone to volunteer any information. In fact, I was surprised Joann had.

"So?" Pam reported. "So, you are the only one with a personal connection?"

"You did it!" Denise accused, pointing a trembling finger at Joann.

"We should tie her up somewhere before she kills us all," Tammy said.

"This is insane," Joann snapped, her voice rising.

"Is it?" Regina shot back, crossing her arms. "You knew him personally. That makes you the prime suspect. And no one else here knew him. You said so yourself."

"We don't know that for sure," Joann shot back.

Kelly set a hand on her hip. "Then why did you say it?"

"I just assumed it since I've never met any of you before at any of Alexander's functions." Joann shrugged before she took another sip of her brandy.

"And you've been to *all* of them?" Regina's tone sounded more like an accusation than a question.

"Of course not," Joann answered.

Bonnie shook her head. "Wait, how did you know him?"

"Must have been his girlfriend. That's why she's so sure she never saw any of us," Heather answered.

Joann slammed her brandy glass down on the table, some of the liquid sloshing out of it. "That's not true. I wasn't his girlfriend. I wasn't romantically involved with him. I was his business partner."

"And how did that relationship end?" Dawn asked.

I stared at Joann, waiting for her response. She seemed nice on the boat over. Friendly. Was it all hiding a big secret? A deadly one?

"I didn't kill him, if that's what you're all getting at."

"Says you," Kelly cried. "How do we know? So far, you're the only one who's had a personal relationship with him. You're the most practical suspect."

"That's not entirely true," I said with a shake of my head.

"Oh, you knew him, too?" Pam asked.

I curled my fingers into fists behind my back, trying to keep my frustration in check. Tempers were running high, and everyone was looking to feel safer—or hide their own guilt—by pointing the finger elsewhere.

"I didn't, no. But what I mean is just because Joann knew him doesn't mean she's the most likely suspect. Anyone here could have killed him for any reason. Clearly, everyone had a reason for coming tonight," I answered.

Joann bobbed her head, poking a finger at me. "Yes, good point, Charlie."

"Wait a minute," Tammy said. "Didn't I see you two talking on the boat?"

Pam's eyes went wider. "Wait, I think I remember that. Yeah, they were talking."

"So, you know each other?" Kelly asked.

"No," I answered with a huff.

Edward crossed the room, waving his glass at me. "Wow, someone sounds defensive."

"I am not!" I shouted.

Joann raised her eyebrows, shaking her head. "Don't sweat it, Charlie. They're looking to string somebody up for this. Just let them foam at the mouths like the rabid dogs they are."

"Rabid dogs?" Pam repeated, her voice incredulous.

Regina scoffed. "Someone's covering guilt."

"Why would I volunteer information if I was covering my guilt?" Joann asked, her arms stretched to the sides.

"To make it look like you're not covering your guilt," Kelly murmured as she wandered past to the drink cart to pour herself another sherry.

"Well, how about someone else goes?" Joann says. "Someone else tell your secret."

"Wait," I said with a wave of my finger in the air, "Heather, you said you knew someone's secret. Was it Joann's?"

"Nope," Heather said with a shake of her head. "I had no idea Joann was Drake's business partner. No, the secret I know is someone else's."

"Whose?" Bonnie demanded. "Tell us what you know."

Heather pressed her lips together and flicked her gaze to Dawn. "When Dawn mentioned that she was a state senator earlier, it triggered my memory. I recognized her, but it didn't click until she mentioned that, and that's when I knew…"

"Knew what?" Tammy asked.

"Dawn isn't a state senator anymore—"

"Because I'm running for something bigger," Dawn interrupted, her voice firm but a hint of panic flickering in her eyes.

Heather shook her head, a small, grim smile tugging at her lips. "No, that's not why. You were forced out, and the reason why… well, let's just say it's not something you'd want on your campaign poster."

My mind was racing. I needed to keep control of the situation, but with every new accusation, the group seemed more on edge. How was I supposed to sort through all these lies and half-truths? Was I even qualified for this? But there was no one else to step up. I had to stay focused, or this would spiral out of control.

CHAPTER 6

 ran a shaky hand through my hair. "Okay, okay, let's just wait a second. Let's all calm down here."

"Why should we listen to you?" Pam asked.

"Because I'm a private investigator. And I think we need some order to this. Accusations are flying around everywhere, and we're not going to be able to glean any details from anything the way this is going."

"So what?" Denise retorted.

"So…unless you're the murderer, I'd think you'd want to solve this and know who is," I shot back, my annoyance growing.

"Oh, so now you're accusing people, huh?" Denise tossed a blonde lock over her shoulder. "Maybe you did it, and you're pointing the fingers everywhere else to deflect."

"I didn't," I growled, "but fine. Does anyone know a secret about me here?"

I slowly spun, searching the group for anyone who wanted to speak up. "Come on. Don't be shy. If someone knows some motive that I'd have, some secret I'm hiding, speak up."

No one said a word.

I arched an eyebrow, lifting my chin. "Yeah, that's what I thought. But it seems everyone else here has a secret. And at least one other person knows about it. So, let's proceed. Heather, tell us what you know."

Heather ran a hand through her copper curls, shifting her weight to one foot. "Dawn left the state senate because she was accused of bribery and corruption."

Gasps went up through the group as all eyes turned to Dawn.

"That's not true," she said with a shake of her head.

"Isn't it?" Heather shot back. "Where did all that money come from then, huh?"

Dawn's features pinched. "What money?"

"You know what money. There were pictures of you on multiple swanky vacations with your family, all of them paid in cash."

"So what?" Dawn shot back. "My husband's a surgeon. We can afford it, though I don't need to explain anything to anyone here."

I crossed my arms, studying her features. The way her eyes shifted, the tension in her muscles, all of it pointed to her being untruthful. "So, you quit the senate to run for something else?"

Dawn pressed her lips together, her jaw tense as she stared at the area rug under her feet. "No, okay? No. I...quit the senate because..."

"Because you took a bribe!" Heather shouted at her.

She shook her head. "No, because I...because...there was a question of my integrity, yes, but I did not take a bribe."

I furrowed my brow. "What?"

"I was...having an affair. That's why we took all the trips. My husband and I were trying to reconnect after it. That's it. I didn't take a bribe, but I didn't want my entire family to deal with the publicity of a politician's infidelity." Dawn sank into a chair as she shook her head.

"So…maybe that's your motive," Tammy said. "Maybe Drake knew about your affair and blackmailed you with it."

"Blackmailed me to what end?" Dawn retorted.

"She has a point," I said. "I mean, her husband knows. He wouldn't have told him."

"He still could have gone public," Kelly said. "Which could ruin any future in politics. She's still a suspect."

I heaved a sigh as I nodded. "Fine, then we have two secrets out, two suspects. Bonnie and Dawn."

"Don't forget Joann. She knew him personally. That makes her a suspect, too."

"Fine." I threw my hands in the air. "Joann is a suspect simply by association."

"No," Joann said. "That's not fair, but either way…we aren't the only three suspects. There's more."

I raised my eyebrows at her. Was she being serious or merely trying to throw the suspicion off of her? It was inter-esting timing that she brought it up right after someone accused her of being a suspect.

Joann seemed nice and sincere when I spoke with her before, but I wondered if I'd been buffaloed by an excellent liar—and a murderer.

"So, you know a secret about someone else?" Regina asked. "What is it?"

"Yes, what is it?" Edward repeated. "I'd love to hear this new turn of events that comes up right after you're accused."

Joann hiked her eyebrows high. "So, you think I'm lying just because someone says I'm a suspect?"

Edward shrugged his shoulders as he poured another brandy. "If the shoe fits."

"The shoe fits every single person here," Joann shot back, her voice sharp as she jabbed a finger at the floor. "I'd suspect we all have a secret. Alexander didn't invite a few random people here because he felt like having a fun time. Every one of us is here for a reason. And knowing Alexander, it's a reason we didn't like."

"Has he done this before?" I inquired.

Joann tossed back the rest of her drink before she stalked across the room to the drink cart. "Not to my knowledge. At least not anything like this. But I do know he somehow found out about people's secrets, and he loved to use them against people to get what he wanted."

"Doesn't look like that worked out for him this time," Kelly said, folding her arms over her chest.

"No, it doesn't," Joann answered, staring into space as she took a sip of her brandy. "This time he bit off more than he could chew. And one of you killed him over it."

Her fingers curled into a fist, and she pounded it against the drink cart, rattling the glasses and decanters as her features twisted.

A tear rolled down her cheek, and she drew in a shaky breath.

"Are you crying?" Heather asked, her voice incredulous.

Joann licked her lips, flicking the tear away. "Well, a man I knew, I mean I was business partners with is dead. Excuse me for having an emotional reaction."

"Or a fake one so we all think that you cared and didn't kill him," Denise said.

"I'm not the actress here, that would be Regina." Joann sniffled and crossed back to her chair, slumping into it with a heavy sigh.

Thunder rumbled overhead, lightning streaking through the sky. The lights flickered again before finally, they went out, plunging us into darkness.

Shrieks went up through the group again. Air rushed past me, fingers brushed my arm.

"E-everyone stay calm!" I called, though my voice shook. "No one move!"

"I want to move," Kelly cried. "Because I want to stay alive. There's a murderer in this room, and we have no idea who could be the next victim."

I swallowed hard, trying to dislodge the lump in my throat. "Okay, we need to find a flashlight or—"

A flame lit across the room. Edward's face glowed as he held it closer before he thrust it into the large fireplace, lighting the kindling under the logs. "This fire should provide us with enough light to see for now."

The flames leapt higher and higher as the kindling burned and caught the logs. The wood crackled as it glowed to life, providing both light and warmth to the room.

I scanned the room, counting each face, my heart pounding in my chest. Ten. We were all still here. Relief washed over me, but it was fleeting. Who among us could be hiding such a dark truth? Could it be the one who looked the most innocent? Or the one who was the quietest? My instincts screamed at me to stay sharp, to question every-thing. I wasn't just a bystander in this twisted game—I had to solve it, or I might be the next one to end up on the wrong side of a knife. "We're all still here and alive."

I bit into my lower lip, realizing that was a miracle in itself. Although, killing someone at this moment may point directly to the killer. I wondered if anyone would be that foolish.

"We should lock the doors!" Kelly shouted. "So no one can get in or out."

"That's stupid," Pam shot back. "We're locking ourselves in with a killer."

"But we're also making sure a killer doesn't get out." Kelly huffed at her, shaking her head.

"But that person could just kill us all."

"In the light? We could easily tackle them." Kelly stamped a foot on the floor.

"Unless the light dies off because we have no more wood because we can't get out because you locked us in," Pam answered with a roll of her eyes. "Use your head."

Kelly wrinkled her nose at the woman, a frown forming on her lips.

"I can't believe you're this worried," Joann said. "You could be the killer."

"I am not!" Kelly shouted.

Joann shrugged. "Says you. Yet you have a secret, too."

"Umm, no." Kelly shook her head, grabbing a lock of her brunette hair to wrap around her fingers.

"Umm, yeah," Joann said with raised eyebrows. "I know your secret, Kelly. I can't believe no one else knows this."

Kelly screwed up her face, shaking her head. "I don't have a secret. I don't, okay? There's no big secret."

Joann offered her a coy smile. "Do you really want to keep playing this game so that once everyone knows, you look like the liar and probably the murderer?"

Kelly's features pinched, her fingers curling into fists. I studied her features closely. She was definitely upset, but was it because she didn't want her secret out, or was it because she was guilty?

"I'm not the murderer!" Kelly shouted before she covered her face with her hands, sobbing. "I didn't do anything wrong."

As Kelly broke down, I couldn't help but feel a pang of sympathy. But was it genuine, or was she trying to deflect attention? The room was like a powder keg, and any spark could set it off. I had to stay focused, but the more secrets that came out, the more tangled this whole mess became.

Bonnie crossed to her and snaked an arm around her shoulders, guiding her to the couch to take a seat. "Shh, it's okay. We all have a secret, honey. It doesn't make any of us murderers."

She narrowed her eyes at Joann. "And if you have something to say, why don't you just say it instead of torturing the poor girl?"

"Fine," Joann said with a shrug, "I just thought she'd want to confess it herself. Sweet little Kelly Culpepper isn't quite so sweet. She may be an heiress, but she couldn't wait for her daddy to keel over to get her money...no, no."

Joann rose from her chair with a slow shake of her head. "No, she wanted her payday early."

Joann stopped in front of Kelly, and Kelly raised her tear-stained cheeks to the woman.

"So, Kelly tried to orchestrate a hostile takeover of her own father's company, so she could cash in early."

The flames in the fireplace cast flickering shadows across the room, making everyone's expressions seem more sinister. Kelly's hands trembled as she buried her face in them, her sobs echoing in the tense silence. Joann's eyes were cold as she delivered her accusation, her voice steady but laced with contempt.

Kelly's features twisted as she stared at Joann. "That's not exactly what happened."

"Isn't it?" Joann asked. "I was approached during your little coup attempt. I thought it stunk what you were doing to your own father who built that company."

"Built it? Well, he's also running it into the ground!" she shouted. "I'll be lucky if I have an inheritance left when he's done. I did what I had to do to try to salvage Culpepper Enterprises."

"So you say. From the outside looking in, it looked like you tried to rob your own father of his company," Joann shot back. "And maybe you robbed Alexander Drake of his life to protect that secret."

"I did not!" Kelly's voice cracked as she shouted, her desperation seeping through. "And besides, I'm not the only one here with a sideways business deal. Someone else may have killed to keep some other business out of the news. And I know just who that is."

I arched my eyebrow, glancing around to see if anyone picked up on her words, but most people kept neutral expressions on their faces. Who else had a secret story to tell?

CHAPTER 7

"More secrets, huh?" Bonnie said with a sigh, her fingers curling into fists as she shook her head. "I'm getting tired of this."

"Well, get over it," Joann retorted as she retook her seat across the room. "We've only been through half of the secrets so far. And there's still a room full of us to go."

Dawn heaved a sigh. "And for those of us who have been outed…we deserve to hear what the rest of you are hiding." She poked a finger at each of the people who hadn't yet been outed.

I glanced at every one of them, trying to assess their reactions. Did Edward flinch? Had there been a flicker of guilt in Regina's eyes?

Or was it Dawn—a woman who wanted the other's secrets exposed—who was trying to hide her guilt?

"Well," Joann answered. "Ask Kelly. She has the next piece of information, according to her."

"Yeah, funny," Heather answered. "She's about to point the finger at someone else after her own greed was outed."

"It wasn't my greed," Kelly said through clenched teeth. "I

was trying to make a smart business move, to save my family's legacy, but never mind. I'm not just pointing the finger to get eyes off me. Because I'm *not* guilty."

"Says you," Tammy retorted with a flick of her strawberry blonde hair. "To me, it reeks of desperation."

"Really?" Kelly shouted back, leaping to her feet, her fists tight at her sides. "What reeks more of desperation? Sitting here hiding your secrets so no one knows you're guilty or openly facing them?"

"All right, all right," I said with a shake of my head as I stepped between them. "Let's all settle down, please. We all know everyone has a secret. I don't think it's that desperate to out someone's secret. We're all trying to get to the bottom of this."

"Except one of us," Pam said. "One of us wants their secret buried. One of us is a murderer."

Thunder boomed overhead again, shaking the glass in the panes as it echoed and rumbled in the distance.

I stiffened my muscles, trying to stop the shiver snaking down my spine from shaking me all over. The fact that I stood in a room that contained a murderer made me nervous. Would they strike again?

"I think we should get the secrets out. All of them," I said. "Because whoever did this could strike again. They could kill someone else who knows their secret. We don't want to risk that."

"That's why I said we should lock the doors," Kelly said as she eased onto the couch.

"What we should do," Pam said, "is go to our rooms and hole up there until we can get off of this island. *That's* how we'll stay safe."

"She's right," Regina said. "That's the only way we'll be safe. Where no one can get to us. Everyone in their own room."

I shook my head. "No. There's no way everyone will stay in their room. People have to come out at some point."

"The only person who *has* to come out is the murderer. They will have to kill the person who knows their secret. The person who leaves their room is the murderer." Pam shrugged her shoulders. "Perfect."

"No," I said with a shake of my head.

"Yeah, what if I'm hungry, and I sneak out for some cheese," Denise asked. "I'm not a murderer because I want a snack."

"Denise has a point," Joann said. "We can't assume because someone left their room. And then it's going to come down to people just hiding out in there, refusing to leave so they aren't considered the murderer."

"I don't see why not," Heather retorted. "It's a perfectly good strategy to me."

"Of course it is," Bonnie shot back. "You haven't had your secret outed yet. Nor has Regina. Everyone with their secret still intact thinks this is a great idea because it makes sure no one can tell on them."

"Unless one of us leaves our room to go to someone else's and tell the secret," Kelly said. "And then we'll be considered a murderer."

"Fine," Regina said with a sharp tone as she collapsed into her seat. "Proceed."

"No!" Heather said with a shake of her head. "No, I think we should go to our rooms and lock ourselves in. I don't want someone to murder me."

"No one wants to be murdered," I answered. "But I don't think locking ourselves in our rooms is going to prevent that."

"Why?" Edward asked. "Are you going to break down our doors and kill us?"

I poked a finger at my chest, my frustration growing. "I

didn't murder anyone. I'm just trying to be an impartial party here. I am a private investigator. This has to be the reason Mr. Drake invited me."

"So you say," Dawn growled. "But for all we know, you're just hiding behind this persona, so no one accuses you of murder."

"I'm not. I have my PI license upstairs. Would it help if I got it?"

Dawn began to nod, and I backed toward the door until Edward blocked me, slamming a hand against the door jamb, his features taut.

"I don't think so," he said.

"What?" I questioned, my features twisting with confusion.

"You're not leaving this room."

"I'm with Edward on this," Pam said, crossing her arms. "No one leaves."

"Yeah, you're probably just trying to get away. Lock yourself in your room and let the rest of us duke it out," Regina shouted.

"All right, well, if someone wants to see my license, we can *all* walk up to my room, and I can get it."

"Should we move?" Kelly questioned. "I mean…if we move, someone could kill someone."

"How?" Joann asked. "We'll all be together."

"Someone will be at the back of the pack. And the murderer can just stay at the back and kill us off one by one," Kelly said.

"It's not that far of a walk," Bonnie said, creasing her forehead.

"Far enough that someone could get killed," Denise said.

"We can't stay in here for the entire weekend," I argued. "We're going to go to bed at some point."

"Oh, so you're planning on going to sleep with a murderer in the house?" Tammy asked.

"Of course she is," Edward answered. "Because she's the murderer. She can sleep tight while the rest of us sweat it out."

Dawn pointed a finger at me. "She was probably trying to get away when she went for the license."

"I was not!" I said before I lowered my voice, trying to remain calm. "All right, I won't show you my license, but I am a PI. And I think we should sort through what everyone knows about each other and see if it helps us. Now, Kelly, what do you know?"

Kelly's fists clenched so tightly her knuckles turned white. Her eyes darted around the room, as if searching for an escape, but there was none. She knew there was no turning back now. "Maybe I shouldn't say," she muttered, but the defiance in her tone was fading, replaced by fear.

Frustration boiled inside me, my jaw flexing. "Are you joking? You insisted you had a secret about someone and now you don't want to say?"

"You're really interested in making sure people's secrets come out, aren't you?" Denise asked.

I slid my eyes closed. "No. I'm not. I don't want people's secrets out. I'm just trying to get to the bottom of this."

"She's right. We're all curious to know the other secrets," Joann said.

Pam slapped her thigh. "Of course you'd defend her. You two know each other."

"We do not," Joann said with a sigh.

"Maybe we should take a vote," Tammy said with a shrug. "See what the majority of us wants to do."

"Fine," I answered. "That's not a bad idea. There are eleven of us, so we need six to win. Who thinks we should—"

"Wait a minute," Regina answered with a shake of her

head, "we should do this with a secret ballot. People are going to feel pressured otherwise."

"Fine," I answered. "Is there any paper?"

People searched the drawers of the tables in the room, Denise finding a notepad and a few pens. I tore a few pages into pieces and handed them out along with the pens to the first few.

"All right. Write your choice on your slip. Write 'Share Secrets' or 'Don't Share.' Fold the paper in half longways." I glanced around the room, finding a bowl. "And put it in this bowl."

Nods met my instructions, and the first set of people with pens scrawled down their choices, quickly folding their papers and holding them close so others couldn't see.

Pens switched hands and the next group jotted down their vote. Kelly handed me her pen, and I scribbled my choice to share the secrets.

I tossed my vote into the bowl and wandered around the room, collecting the others votes.

"Make sure you mix them up," Pam said. "So we don't know whose is whose."

I bobbed my head, reaching my hand into the porcelain object to stir up the votes. I pulled out the first one. "First vote is not to share."

My stomach clenched as I worried that I may be outvoted. I wanted to know more about these people to see if I could nail down a motive and determine who was a killer.

"Second vote…" I reached into the bowl and pulled out another slip of paper. "Share."

"So we're one to one," Kelly said with a nod.

"Great job keeping track, genius," Dawn muttered under her breath, casting a sideways glance at Kelly.

Bonnie shook her head. "There's no need for that."

I continued, grabbing another few papers out of the bin

and opening them. "All right, we have two more not shares, and one more share."

"Six votes to go," Pam announced.

I grabbed three more papers and opened them. "All right, two more not shares, and one more share."

"So, if we get one more vote not to share, we're done here," Tammy said, crossing her arms.

I tried to keep my features impartial as I nodded. "Right."

I pulled out the next slip and opened it, my hands shaking as I wondered if I'd get voted down. "Share."

I hadn't gotten to my vote yet, so I knew there was one more share in the bowl. But were there two? Would I win?

I pulled out the next paper and opened it, recognizing my handwriting. "Share." I blew out a long sigh. "One vote left."

With my breath held, I fished out the last paper, pressed my lips together, and unfurled it. My eyes slid closed for second.

"Well?" Edward demanded.

I twisted it toward the group. "Share."

Joann rose. "Well, that's six to five to share. Looks like Kelly's on."

Tammy waved a hand in the air. "Whoa, that was a close vote. I think we should try again."

"No," I insisted. "The group decided to vote and agreed to go with the majority. We share. Joann's right. Kelly, tell us what you know."

I crossed my arms, aiming my gaze at Kelly as I wondered what secret she may reveal. Who else had a motive to kill someone?

CHAPTER 8

elly's hands trembled as all eyes turned toward her. She sank into her seat again, slouching down a little.

"Well, come on," Joann said. "We voted. Spit it out."

"Give her a second," Bonnie said, wrapping an arm around Kelly and rubbing her shoulder. "Take your time, honey."

"Who is it about?" Pam asked. "Start there."

Kelly raised a trembling finger and pointed across the room. All eyes followed the trajectory of her point. "Edward."

He pulled his chin back to his chest. "What? What kind of lie are you about to spin about me?"

"It's not a lie," Kelly shot back. "I know what you did. I overheard a few people talking about how you 'helped them out.'"

Her features twisted into an upset frown as she said the words. "But you ruined so many people."

"Doing what?" Regina asked.

"Manipulating stock prices," Kelly answered. "He did some of his cronies a few favors, ensuing their stock got pumped up way more than it should have. They cashed out rich before it crashed. People lost their entire portfolios."

"I never told them not to diversify. I can't be held responsible for this," Edward shot back.

"So you did it?" Dawn asked.

"I didn't say that. I'm not admitting to anything. But the people who cried that they lost everything when those stock prices crashed should have been better invested." Edward shrugged, brushing off the accusation.

Many of the others seemed upset when they'd been accused of wrong doing, but Edward seemed to blame others. Did that mean he'd do the same with a murder? Could he easily put it behind him as someone else's fault?

I narrowed my eyes at him, searching for any sign of guilt. Could he have stabbed our host? If Drake had any proof of the stock price manipulation, he could have. It would cost Edward everything. He also had the means to wedge a knife that deep into a man's back.

But likely so did many of the ladies here. I couldn't accuse him simply because he lacked remorse for a crime he didn't even admit to.

The suspect list was growing with every accusation, and we still had many more to go. Would someone crack under the pressure and confess? Or would I end up with ten suspects and no clues?

"All right, so he manipulated stock prices and cost people a mint. But would that be enough to drive him to murder? What if Drake had proof? Proof that could ruin him, destroy his career, and send him to prison. Could Edward have decided that silencing Drake was his only way out?" Pam asked, her voice tinged with suspicion.

"Could be," Bonnie shot back. "He's in banking. He could be banned from it."

"So, if this got out, he'd lose his job," Joann said, her gaze narrowing on Edward. "And maybe he thought losing his job wasn't the worst of it. What if Drake threatened to expose him? That's a motive, all right. Just like Bonnie's plagiarism could've ended her career, Dawn's affair could've destroyed her family, and Kelly's takeover attempt could ruin her father. Any of us could have seen murder as the only way to protect our secrets."

"I didn't do it!" Kelly said. "I'd hardly kill someone over my secret."

"We don't know that's true," Pam said.

"Okay, so we've heard five secrets," I answered, trying to keep this on track. "Does anyone else know anything about anyone else in the room?"

Silence stretched between us before Dawn slowly raised her hand. "I do."

All eyes turned to her, and she shook her blonde hair, lifting her chin. "I recognized someone when I came in. I'd seen her a number of times before."

"Who?" Pam demanded.

Dawn licked her lips before she flicked her gaze to Tammy and pointed. "Her."

Tammy shifted her weight from foot to foot. "Me? What do you think you know about me?"

"You're a reporter. I recognized you from being at some of my events."

"Being a reporter's not a crime. At least, I didn't think so," Tammy retorted.

Joann crossed her arms. "The way they report the news these days, maybe it should be."

"What's that supposed to mean?" Tammy asked, her fingers curling into fists.

"It means if I click on one more clickbait headline," Heather said, "I'm going to scream. Especially when it's followed by some half-baked article that's barely readable."

"Oh, well," Dawn said with a shrug. "You had that almost right. Her articles are readable, but they're not even baked. They're not even true!"

"What?" Tammy shrieked, her eyes going wide. "How dare you impugn my reputation like that?"

"Oh, honey you did that yourself when you fabricated a news story." Dawn rolled her eyes.

"I did not," Tammy said, her fingers curling into fists.

"What did she make up?"

"Remember *Children of War?*" Dawn crossed her arms, lifting her chin as she stared at Tammy. "All fake. Those kids in the article weren't even from that war-torn country. She had them made-up, had them photographed, manipulated the photographs, and made up the entire story."

Gasps went up through the room as people reacted to the news of the journalist faking a story.

"That's awful. Shame on you," Kelly said.

"Oh, who did it hurt? There are plenty of children of war who would have had that exact experience. It wasn't a fabrication."

"Except it was. A bill came across my desk for aid to be sent to that country. We sent *millions* because of that story, and it was all fake. I didn't get the chance to out it before I had to step down. You manipulated our budgets. And you could lose your credentials if it ever got out."

Tammy licked her lips. "No one can prove anything, and I'm not saying I did it."

"You did it, all right. And maybe now you killed to keep it quiet."

Tammy crossed her arms, flicking her gaze out the window. "I'm finished with you people. You jump to conclusions all over the place. You just accused Edward not five minutes ago, and now you're accusing me. And there are plenty more people to have their secrets outed. Including Regina, our resident celebrity."

Regina's eyes went wide at the accusation, and she pressed a hand to her chest. "Me? Why I'm an open book. I have nothing to hide. Everyone knows everything about me."

"Everything except what you did to get where you are," Tammy retorted.

Regina scoffed. "I don't know what you *think* you know, but none of it is true."

"Isn't it? We should ask Olivia Green about that."

"Who?" Denise questioned, her features pinching.

Tammy poked a finger at her. "Exactly. No one's heard of her, am I right?"

Head shakes answered her question.

"No, I didn't think so. That's because sweet Regina here ruined her way back when to make sure *she* got offered the big roles."

"That's not true!" Regina shouted.

"Ohh, someone's touchy about this," Tammy said with a smirk. "And it's absolutely true. You want to accuse me of making up stories, fine. But this one is very true. She made certain that Ms. Green got caught with drugs—drugs she planted."

Exclamations went up through the group as Tammy made the accusation.

"It's not true!"

She seemed convincing, but she was an actress. I'd have to take every reaction with a grain of salt.

Regina sniffled, a lone tear falling to her cheek. "But it's fine. I'm used to hurtful comments. Being a celebrity, you have to develop a tough skin. But I certainly never did any such thing."

"Yeah, right," Heather said with a roll of her eyes. "We all know you'd do *anything* to get ahead."

"You're one to talk," Regina said with a guffaw. "After what you did."

Heather tugged her chin back to her chest. "What's that supposed to mean?"

"It's supposed to mean your hands aren't lily white, either. I know what you did."

Kelly cocked her head, her eyebrows furrowing. "Well, tell us, so we know, too."

Regina rose, standing stick straight as she lifted her chin. "Certainly. Ms. Heather Baker claims to be an art dealer…but she sells fake art."

"What?" Heather asked, her eyes blazing.

"Mm-hmm," Regina said with a curt nod. "A friend of mine bought something from you. He fell on some hard times, went to sell it, and found out it was a fake. So, you see, you're not so far from the rest of us, are you?"

"I can't believe anybody would put stock in anything that's coming out tonight. It's all false. All of it."

"I have the proof, honey," Regina said with an arch of her eyebrow.

"It seems we all have proof of something else someone has done," Joann answered. "And I can almost guarantee that's exactly what Alexander expected. He meant to turn us against each other."

"Except…no one seems to have turned against you, Pam, or Denise." Heather said with a tilt of her head.

Pam stepped forward, the flames of the dying fire making her face look more sinister than it had before. "I know Denise's secret."

Denise rose, her body trembling as she glared at Pam. "And I know yours."

"Maybe we ought to both keep quiet," Pam suggested, crossing her arms.

"No, no," Heather said with a shake of her head. "We all agreed to tell, so one of you speak up."

"She's unethical," they both said at the same time, poking fingers at each other.

"Okay, whoa, one at a time," I said, waving my hands in the air.

"Oh, here we go. The private investigator who wants to pretend she's a cop would like law and order, folks," Dawn said.

I clicked my tongue, taking a breath to calm myself. "That's not true, but you both have something to say, and I think we'd all like to hear each secret."

"Fine, I'll go first," Denise said. "Pam conducted a variety of unethical experiments last year, withholding treatments from patients in order to assess how a disease progressed."

"That's how all experiments work!" Pam cried.

"It's not. You can't withhold treatment from sick people. You told them they'd be receiving the current standard of care, but you gave them sugar pills! Some of those people died because of you. Your credentials could be stripped! You'd lose everything if this got out. So you killed just one more, didn't you?"

"I did not. But you did. You've killed someone, too, didn't you, *doctor*?'

"That was a terrible accident."

"It was malpractice," Pam shot back. "She was drunk in the OR! We all know it. And I'd bet Mr. Drake could've proved it. So she had all the reason in the world to kill him."

"But I didn't," Denise said. "Maybe she did."

Denise jabbed her finger at Joann.

"I already told you I knew him. I made no secret of it."

"No," Edward answered from a dark corner. "But you have one other secret, too, don't you?"

"I don't know what you're talking about." Joann shrugged, her finger tracing the rim of her glass.

"Don't you?" Edward asked. "You knew Alexander, you were his business partner...who embezzled from his company. That's what led to your falling out."

Joann huffed a chuckle out. "I didn't do that."

"Wow, double motive!" Kelly said. "You knew him *and* you stole from him. You probably did it."

"I did not! He was my friend. I didn't kill him," Joann shouted.

Arguments broke out all over the room, with people accusing each other of killing our host until I finally couldn't take anymore.

"Enough!" I shouted. "That is enough! Now, everyone here has a secret. And everyone's secret has been exposed. One of you is the killer. But we're no closer to figuring that out. So I would recommend that instead of accusing each other at random, we all let this information settle and go to our rooms for the night."

"We should settle in. It's getting late, and we're not getting anywhere," Joann said, but I barely heard her.

My mind was spinning, replaying the night's events, trying to make sense of the chaos. Everyone here had a reason to be afraid, but fear alone doesn't drive someone to kill. Desperation does. I needed to find out who was the most desperate, who had the most to lose. Because that's where I'd find the killer.

"Says the killer," Heather shot back.

"I am not the killer, and I'm not going to put up with any more of this. I'll be locked in my room. Good night." Joann strode away, leaving the rest of us behind.

One by one, the others retreated to their rooms, the tension in the air thick enough to cut. I lingered by the dying fire, watching the embers glow and fade, my mind racing.

Someone in this house was desperate—desperate enough to kill. The secrets we'd uncovered were dangerous, but I knew there was more, something deeper that we hadn't touched on yet. I could feel it, like a storm gathering on the horizon. And when it hit, I had a sinking feeling that someone else wouldn't survive the night.

I pushed away from the fireplace, my thoughts churning. I needed to think, to piece together the puzzle before it was too late. But as I turned to leave the room, a faint noise caught my attention—a creak on the floor above, a door softly closing. My heart skipped a beat. Was someone moving around in the darkness, setting the stage for another murder? I had to find out. Quietly, I slipped out of the room and into the shadows, determined to catch the killer before they could strike again.

CHAPTER 9

I hesitated on the step, my fingers curling around the ornate railing as I stared upstairs. I should go straight to my room, but the private investigator in me wanted to search for more clues. If I wasn't mistaken, our host's death wasn't the end of the trouble.

I couldn't glean any details from the secrets revealed after we'd discovered the body. All of them had a motive, maybe some more so than others, but that didn't mean the ones with more to lose definitely killed him.

All of them stood to lose something, and any of them could have killed him.

I chewed my lower lip, flicking my gaze to the floor above me. No sounds floated down. Was everyone in their rooms?

It was likely the case, but for how long would that be? I didn't expect everyone to stay put all night. Someone would panic for one reason or another. Either they'd be afraid they heard something and hurry to someone else's room, or they'd be worried someone would finger them for the crime.

I needed more information. Much more. I needed to have

a good idea if someone came knocking on my door whether or not they could be a killer or a friend.

With a heavy sigh, I eased my foot slowly down to the marble floor, wincing as my sneaker squeaked.

With a glance over my shoulder, I hurried to the dining room and used my trusty lockpick kit to unlock the door. My fingers wrapped around the cold brass handle, and I turned it inch by inch, another grimace escaping me as the hinges creaked.

I cursed under my breath as I slipped inside and eased the door closed, another protest coming from the rusty hinges.

My lower lip trembled as I shot a glance over my shoulder at the dead body still slumped over at the head of the table. I lifted my chin, swallowing hard. I needed to buck up. I had to search for clues.

I crept forward, closer to the body. Every groan of the house sent my heart rate spiraling higher and higher. As I reached him, I leaned closer to study the knife. Even if there were fingerprints, I couldn't see them.

But I doubted there were. All of these people knew why they were here. They could have easily premeditated this crime. In that case, they'd likely have worn gloves.

I studied the angle of the knife, attempting to determine if it was a left-handed person or a right-handed person.

We only had two lefties in the group. I pulled my trusty notepad from my purse and quickly jotted down that Regina and Bonnie were both lefties, at least that was how they'd written their votes, and none of them looked scrawled.

I snapped a few pictures from various angles, trying to determine the angle the person would have to use. I raised my right hand and brought it down, then tried with my left.

It appeared that a righty had done the deed, effectively ruling out Regina and Bonnie from my suspect list. But that left eight others.

I glanced down at the blood that dripped onto the chair and floor, searching it for any hairs that could be used to help identify the suspect, but I found none.

With a sigh, I returned my attention to the body. I grimaced, removing a tissue from my purse. It wasn't much, but it would have to be enough.

Carefully, with my fingers wrapped in the tissue, I shifted the body back.

A shiver shook me, and I groaned as I stared at his face, frozen in a shocked expression. He'd already started to turn pale, almost blue. His skin looked cold and disgusting.

With my handy hanky, I reached for his jacket pocket, my nose wrinkled at the idea of searching a dead body.

Before I could do anything, a voice startled me.

"What are you doing?"

My eyes went wide, and I spun around in a circle, staring in the direction of the voice. I swallowed hard, pressing my hand against my chest.

My breath hitched as Kelly appeared in the doorway, her silhouette a shadowy figure against the dim light. Could she have returned to destroy evidence? Was I about to become her next victim? I tightened my grip on the tissue-wrapped knife handle, ready to defend myself if necessary.

I lost the ability to breathe, wondering if she was the killer.

"Kelly!" I shouted.

"Yeah?" Her features twisted as her gaze flicked between me and the body. "Oh no. Are you the killer? Are you going to kill me?"

"What?" I asked. "No! No, I'm…what are you doing here? I could ask you the same question."

"I'm not the killer. I told you that." She wrung her hands as she grimaced at me. "But I was worried the killer would come and kill me, so I went to your room, but you didn't answer. Then I heard a noise down here, so I came down to check it out."

"Oh," I said with a nod. I hadn't ruled Kelly out yet, but it made sense. Although, I still didn't trust her. "Well, you should go back upstairs and lock your door. You shouldn't be roaming around the house."

Suddenly, Kelly gasped, her arms flailing in the air as she raced into the room and hid behind me. "Someone's coming!"

"What?" I whispered, my heart hammering against my ribs.

"I heard footsteps," she hissed.

I wondered if I could make it to the door and back to close it before they arrived. But before I could decide, Joann appeared in the doorway.

Her jaw dropped open as she spotted us. "Charlie? Kelly?"

"We're investigating," Kelly said with a raise of her chin.

"Why wasn't I asked? He was my friend," Joann said.

I stepped forward. "Actually, I was investigating, then Kelly came in. She was too afraid to stay alone."

"Or she killed him."

Kelly jabbed a finger at Joann. "Or you did. You're here, too."

"I was here because he was my friend. I was going to say goodbye. But if we're investigating, I want in."

I shook my head. "We're not investigating. I was investigating. You should—"

"I'm not leaving," Joann said, shaking her head and crossing her arms.

"Me either," Kelly mimicked, matching her stance.

I clicked my tongue. "No. No! You two are suspects. I can't—"

"I'm *not* the killer," Joann answered. "And to be fair, I don't think Kelly is either."

"Aw, thank you. Well, I think Joann is way too nice to be the killer," Kelly said with a smile.

"You can't just rule each other out because you were nice to each other. We need actual clues."

"Have you found any?" Joann asked.

I lifted a shoulder in a shrug. "Maybe. But I'm not sharing."

"All right," Joann said. I could call everyone down here. Tell them the investigation is on. Then we can all search for clues."

I slid my eyes closed. I was being blackmailed. Did that make it more likely that she was the killer? Probably not. She wouldn't want to call a ton of people down here if she was. Someone may find a clue, and she also wouldn't be able to kill anyone else. Kelly and I were easier targets on our own without a group of people surrounding us.

A battle raged in my mind—was I making a mistake by letting them in? I needed all the help I could get, but the more people involved, the less control I had. And control was crucial if I was going to survive this night.

"Fine, fine," I said with a shake of my head. "The only observation I've made so far is that it appears the knife was wielded by a right-handed person."

Joann tried to glance at the knife in Alexander Drake's back. "All right. That rules out Regina and Bonnie."

Kelly wrinkled her nose at the assessment as I nodded. "How?"

"They both used their left hands to write their votes earlier. If this was a right-handed person, it isn't one of them."

"Oh," Kelly said with a nod. "Got it. What else?"

"Nothing," I answered. "I was just about to search his pockets, but then you two showed up."

Joann waved a hand at the body. "Go ahead."

I pressed my lips together, a lump forming in my throat. "Ugh, okay. Here it goes."

"Seriously?" Joann asked.

Kelly frowned. "I'm with Charlie. It's gross."

"Give me the tissue," Joann said, holding her hand out.

"I really should do it myself…" I flicked my gaze back to the body, my stomach flip-flopping before I finally thrust the tissue at Joann. "Thanks."

She slid her hand into his outer breast pocket, shaking her head. "Nothing."

After shifting him a little, she tried his side pockets, then his pants pockets. "Not a thing."

"There's an inside pocket on his left side," Kelly said.

"I know," Joann answered. "I was building up to that. That's…grosser."

"What if we take his jacket off?" Kelly suggested.

"How do we get around the knife?" Joann asked.

"Oh." Kelly frowned. "Yeah. Ummm, we could just open it and hold it out?"

We agreed on that compromise, and I flipped up a piece of his jacket to undo the button without touching it, then held it out.

Joann sucked in a deep breath before she dove into the pocket. Her lips parted, and she held a finger in the air. "There's something in there."

"What?" Kelly asked.

She shrugged. "I don't know. It's hard, cold, odd shaped. I'm trying to get a hold of it, but this tissue leaves something to be desire."

She fished around for a few more seconds. "Stop shifting his jacket."

"Sorry," I said, "I can't help it. My hands are shaking." I made a conscious effort to hold my hands steady while she pressed her lips together, digging into the pocket. "I got it. I got it!"

She grinned as she lifted an object triumphantly from within his pocket.

I dropped his jacket, a shiver snaking down my spine before I focused on the object in her hand. In the dim light of the dying candles, I spotted a brass key.

Ornate, with intricate carvings etched into its bow. It was heavier than I expected, the kind of key that opened something important, something old. But what? My mind raced with possibilities. Was this the key to a hidden room? A safe? Or maybe it unlocked a secret none of us were prepared to face.

We had to figure out what it opened. And we had to do it fast before anyone could remove any other pieces of evidence.

CHAPTER 10

$\mathcal{I}$ stared at the brass key, my heart hammering in my chest as I studied it. Would it lead us to anything or be another dead end?

I reached for it, but Joann pulled it back, sending my heart plummeting. Had she tricked us?

Was she merely here to find the key so she could suppress any evidence against herself?

Was she the killer?

My heart rose into my throat as my gaze slid around the space in search of a weapon. I wondered for a brief moment if I could yank the knife from Drake's back and use it against her.

Ironic, the killer killed by her own murder weapon.

"Look, Joann," I said when I couldn't find any other options to defend myself, "Let's talk about this."

"Talk about what? It's obvious."

I winced. "I don't think it is. I don't think anyone would know. I didn't know."

"Well, you should," she shot back. "You're a PI for heaven's sake."

"I know." I shrugged, trying to act innocent. "That's what I mean. I'm a PI, and I didn't figure it out. No one else will either."

Joann heaved a sigh, shaking her head as she wrapped the key tighter in the tissue. "Everyone knows you can't touch evidence." She thrust it toward me, and I stared at it as if it was a bug.

"What?"

"You tried to grab the key. But you can't touch it. It could have fingerprints or something."

My chin lifted as I suddenly understood her reaction. "Ohhh, I thought…"

A chuckle escaped me, and I slapped my thigh.

"What?" Joann crinkled her forehead.

"I thought…" I laughed again. "Oh, this is funny, you're going to laugh. I thought you were here to get that key because you killed him. And that you'd double crossed us."

Kelly joined in my laughter, but Joann arched an eyebrow. "Are you serious? You still think I'm the killer?"

My mind raced, a whirlwind of fear and suspicion. Was Joann really just being cautious, or was she hiding something more sinister? But then, as she handed me the tissue-wrapped key with nothing but concern in her eyes, my fear subsided. Maybe I was letting the tension get to me. I fluffed it off, trying to move forward.

"No, of course not. Just that one blip, you know." I slicked a lock of hair behind my ear as I offered her an awkward grin. "Anyway…we should really figure out what that key goes to."

Joann stared at it again for a second as I took it. "I've seen him with this before, but I don't know what it goes to."

"Maybe a safe. Did he have an office in the house?"

Joann nodded. "Yes. I can show you."

I motioned for her to lead us to the room. As she took a

step, I grabbed her arm. "Wait. We should be quiet and discreet. We don't want the others to know we're poking around."

"Okay," she answered softly. "I'll peek into the hall before we move."

We followed her to the door, and I held my breath as I waited for her to give us the all-clear. Joann leaned into the hall, her head swinging back and forth until she gave us a thumbs up signal. "We're going to the right."

We tiptoed into the hall, following her down to another hallway, then to a set of double doors. A set of red, velvet curtains framed it. Why did this door look so familiar?

I didn't have time to think about it any further before Joann whisked the doors open and herded us inside.

With a final glance up and down the hall, I ducked into the ornately decorated office and glanced around. My eyes fell on the Tiffany lamp on the polished mahogany desk. "Wow, he sure liked his luxuries."

"That he did," Joann said as she crossed to a large oil painting of Alexander Drake in an ornate gold frame that rose behind his desk chair. She swung it open, revealing a safe. "It's key coded, not an actual key."

"What about a lock box or something?" Kelly asked.

I poked a finger at her. "Good thought. We should have a look around in here."

We spread out, searching the bookcases, storage spaces, desk, and even picking up the rugs to check for any secret panels in the floor.

"Nothing," I said, spreading out my arms to each side. As the words left my mouth, a noise sounded above us. I swallowed hard as my heart started pounding. The reminder that eight other people—one of them a killer—remained in the house with us shot through my mind.

"We need to quietly continue our search," I said. "We need to figure out who did this."

Kelly chewed her lower lip as she nodded. "But where? What else could that key go to?"

I paced around the room, my forehead creased. "Something is niggling at me, and I don't know what."

"The fact that we're stuck here with a killer, maybe?" Kelly asked.

"Or that we still have six suspects?" Joann added. "And no way to rule any of them out."

I shook my head. "No, but when I saw those curtains, I thought sure this key would go to something in here. Why?"

"Because you figured it would open a safe in his office?" Kelly suggested with a shrug.

"No," I said with another shake of my head.

My mind whirled but seemed to block any meaningful thoughts from forming. "The curtains reminded me of something."

Kelly narrowed her eyes at me. "His fancy taste?"

"No…" I spun on my heel, something finally springing into my mind. I snapped my fingers, twisting to face the other two women. "There's a door upstairs, barely visible. Almost completely covered by red, velvet curtains. Maybe the key goes to something there!"

"We can try it…but we have to be quiet," Joann said. "We'll be dangerously close to the others. We don't want to get caught. It's too dangerous."

"Right. Umm, should we go up together?" I asked.

"Safer in numbers, right?" Kelly said.

"Also, louder."

"But can we go separately and not get caught?"

Joann raised a finger in the air. "There's a set of back stairs. We'll take those. Maybe it'll be easier."

"Great," I said with a bob of my head, "lead the way."

Joann headed for the door to the office, slowly easing it back and peering into the hall. "We're clear. We'll go to the right, past the other hall to a door."

With our trip mapped out, Joann slipped from the room. My heart pounded against my ribs as I glanced down the hall before following her, keeping tight hold of Kelly's hand. We arrived at the door, and Joann threw it open, revealing a steep set of servant stairs.

I winced as we mounted them, and they groaned underneath us. "Are they always this loud?"

"How should I know? I never used them. I just take the main stairs."

"But those go past everyone's bedrooms," Kelly said. "So, let's hope this is the better option."

"With all this creaking, I'm not sure it is," I answered, my heart hammering.

As we reached the top of the stairs, a door blocked us from the hallway. My palms turned sweaty. I swallowed hard as Joann turned the doorknob millimeter by millimeter.

Sweat beaded on my brow as a crack formed. I shifted to peer through the slit, a shaky vision of the hall forming.

Joann quickly tugged the door back. "Someone's out there."

"Who?" I hissed. "It could be a clue."

"Well, maybe not," Kelly whispered. "We were both out, and we're innocent."

"Okay, so then maybe they can rule them out."

Joann shook her head. "I don't know. A blonde. And there are dozens of those here."

Footsteps pounded past us, and my eyes went wide. What would we do if they opened the door? How would we explain what we were doing?

My mind raced as I searched for a reason. We were getting a bottle of wine to try to sleep. We were eating cheese. Why did I come up with that?

I rolled my eyes at myself as the footsteps slowly receded.

"Sounds like they're going back to their room," Joann said.

A few seconds later, a door softly closed.

"Let's go," she said, pushing into the hall and hurrying forward.

I raced after her, dragging Kelly with me.

We rounded the corner, and I banged into the railing that overlooked the stairs, wincing as my hip smarted.

We hurried down the length of the hall as quickly and quietly as possible to the door nearly hidden by the curtains.

The faint scent of old wood and musty velvet filled the narrow hallway. The cold brass key felt heavy in my pocket, almost like it was burning a hole there. Every creak of the floorboards echoed in my ears, making me wince, as if the house itself was conspiring to reveal our presence.

Joann twisted the knob, but it didn't budge. "It's locked!"

"Great!" Kelly whispered. "Now what?"

"Wait, wait!" I fished the key from my pocket. "Maybe this opens it."

Joann grabbed it, the tissue still wrapped around it, and pushed it into the lock. "It fits."

"Hurry," Kelly said, her voice rushed as she bounced on her toes. "Someone's coming!"

"What?" Joann asked as she twisted the key, but it didn't budge.

"Someone's coming. I heard a door!" Kelly exclaimed, her voice barely above a whisper.

"I'm trying, but the key won't go." Joann's hands trembled as she fumbled with the key, sweat beading on her forehead. Each failed attempt ratcheted up the tension, like a clock ticking down to disaster. Kelly was practically vibrating with fear beside me, and I could feel my own panic rising, threatening to overwhelm my reason.

My mind swirled as I wondered who was coming. Was it the killer? Would we be able to overpower them if it was?

"Hurry, Joann," I whispered, though it felt like shouting in the heavy silence.

I shifted my weight from foot to foot as panic raced through me. "If you can't get it, leave it…we'll run to my room. It's right around the corner."

"I can get it. I just need a few seconds," Joann said.

"We don't have a few seconds, we have to go now." I glanced past Kelly, my breath catching in my throat.

"Hurry!" Kelly said.

"I'm trying!" Joann answered through clenched teeth.

"It's not going to work," I said. "Let's go."

Just as I took a step toward the hall, the lock clanked. Joann plowed into the room, grabbing hold of my arm and dragging me backward.

I pulled Kelly with me. We stumbled into the darkened room as someone appeared in the hall. Joann quickly pushed the door almost closed. We all piled closer, staring at the figure in the hall.

A second later, Denise turned toward us, inching forward swiftly and quietly.

My breath hitched, and every muscle in my body tensed as if I'd been struck by lightning. The dim light cast long shadows over her figure, making her seem larger, more menacing. My heart pounded so hard I was sure she could hear it. We huddled together, barely daring to breathe, as she inched closer.

The three of us gasped. Could we be looking at the murderer?

Denise moved with a purpose, her eyes scanning the

hallway like a predator searching for prey. The shadows seemed to swallow her whole, making her approach even more terrifying. My mouth went dry, and I could feel Joann and Kelly stiffen beside me. We were trapped, nowhere to run, nowhere to hide. If Denise was the killer, we were about to find out in the worst possible way.

CHAPTER 11

"She's coming right at us!" Kelly squealed.

"Shhh," both Joann and I said as I clamped a hand over her mouth.

I shifted my gaze back through the slit in the door. Denise flicked her gaze toward us. Had she heard? Would she find the door and come barging in?

I held my breath as she took a few more steps down the hall, looking like she was coming right at us. My mind spun, trying to come up with an explanation for why we were in this room, what we were doing, and whether or not we should trust her if she said she wasn't the killer and wanted to help investigate.

Finally, she veered off, scurrying down another hall away from us.

We all let out a collective sigh, and Joann eased the door completely shut, flicking the lock. "That was too close."

"I know," I said with a nod. "I sure thought she heard us."

"Thank goodness she didn't. Or we'd all be dead proba-bly," Kelly said.

Joann screwed up her face. "You think Denise did it?"

"She's right-handed, so there's a one in six chance she's the killer, and with her roaming around, it may be higher," Kelly answered.

"We're roaming around," I pointed out. "And we didn't do it."

"Good point," Kelly said.

"Well," I answered as I searched the nearby wall for a light switch. "I guess we should look around in here and see if we can find any clues as to who could have done this. Maybe we can confirm some of the stories or refute some and cross people's motives off the list."

The room was steeped in shadows, the air thick with the scent of old books and polished wood. Every creak of the floorboards echoed like a warning, reminding us that we were trespassing in a dead man's secrets.

We all spread out, and I crossed toward the elegantly made four-poster bed. "He really liked his nice stuff, huh?"

"I told you he did," Joann said as she tugged open a drawer on a side table near a setup of armchairs.

After a little rummaging around, she slammed it shut.

"Do you think we'll find anything?" Kelly asked. "I mean… it's not like he could name his murderer, right?"

"No, he couldn't," I answered, tugging back the throw pillows to check behind them. "But maybe we'll rule people out if we can figure out if any of their motives don't actually exist. I mean, a lot of accusations were thrown around, but were all of them true?"

"The one about me was true," Kelly answered as she pulled clothes out of a dresser drawer. "Sadly. I did try a hostile takeover, but like I said, it was to save the company, not to ruin it."

"But does everyone know you set that up and the reason why?"

She shrugged and shook her head. "I'm pretty sure my

dad doesn't know, and I'd hate for him to find out, but…darn it, if he didn't mismanage the company, I wouldn't have had to do it."

I glanced at her, studying the rueful expression on her features. She looked like she genuinely felt bad. Was it all an act? Was this all part of an elaborate plan to find and destroy any evidence against her?

"I know, honey," Joann said as she searched a wardrobe for any clues. "If he doesn't wise up, he's going to drive that company into the ground, but honestly, you've got your own thing. Go with it."

"I know, but it's my legacy, and he's ruined it. The Culpepper name is attached to that."

Joann shot her an apologetic smile. "I know it's a hard pill to swallow, but sometimes, you just need to let it go and move on."

Kelly wrinkled her nose, staring at Joann. "Do you do that?"

"What?" Joann asked, flicking on her cell phone's flashlight and searching the dark corners of the wardrobe.

"Let it go and move on," Kelly said.

"I try to. Easier said than done." She straightened with a sigh. "Nothing in here."

"Could you do it with me?" Her features twisted into a frown. "I…accused you of murder because of the secret about you. But…I shouldn't have. I don't think you did it."

Joann glanced at her, offering her a reassuring smile. "It's okay. Lots of people believe that rumor."

"So…you didn't do it?" Kelly asked.

I shifted my gaze to Joann to gauge her reaction. Would she confess to the crime now in the private room of the victim? Or would she deny it?

Joann lowered her gaze to the floor. "I didn't do it. I took money, that's true. Money owed to me. He called it embezzlement, said I stole it and left. But I have all the proof that it was owed to me. It was a business disagreement."

I narrowed my eyes at her, trying to read any guilt in her face, but I found none.

Kelly seemed to accept the solution, nodding before she returned to her search. "Well, I'm coming up empty, too."

Joann sighed. "Seems like we all are. I'll check the bathroom. Maybe we'll get lucky."

She trod across the floor, a floorboard squeaking as she went. I sank down onto the edge of the bed to wait, wondering if it was creepy that I was sitting on a dead guy's bed.

I decided it wasn't. It wasn't like the dead body was in it. Joann returned from the bathroom, leaning against the jamb. "Nothing in there."

I heaved a sigh, shaking my head. "We were grasping at straws anyway. Like Kelly said, it's not like he wrote down who his killer was."

"No," Joann said, rubbing her arms, "but he usually wrote everything down. So we may have gotten some clues as to whose motives were legitimate."

I furrowed my brow. "What did your letters say?"

Joann tugged a paper from her pocket and unfurled it.

"You brought it?"

"Yep," she answered with a nod before she cleared her throat and read the note. "Congratulations on your financial upturn. Your ambition has not gone unnoticed. I invite you to join me for an exclusive gathering on my private island. It will be an opportunity to discuss mutual interests. Come prepared to confront your past and embrace the future. Your presence is expected, and your compliance is non-negotiable. Failure to meet my demand will result in a less than satisfying conclusion for you."

She folded the note and glanced at me, then Kelly. "How about you two?"

"Mine was about the same," Kelly answered. "Almost identical."

"Mine was a little different," I admitted. "Congratulations on opening your new detective agency. Your ambition has not gone unnoticed. If you would like to start what I am certain will be your illustrious career with a bang, I invite you to my island this weekend for a house party. It is certain to be an illuminating time and a life-changing experience. Bring formal wear for dinners and a weapon. I am certain you will need it. The weapon, that is, though you will need the formal wear, too."

Joann raised her eyebrows. "Did you bring the weapon?"

"Yeah," I said with a nod.

Kelly's eyes went wide. "Wow, really? Good. Then at least we have some protection against the killer."

I winced. "I left it in my room."

Kelly clicked her tongue. "That's silly. Go get it."

"Actually, we could just hole up in her room and try to vet through this," Joann suggested. She crossed toward the room, stepping on the creaky floorboard.

I froze as I rose, my eyebrows furrowing. "Wait...that floorboard..."

"Is going to give us away," Kelly said. "Make sure you don't step on it."

Kelly raised her arms up as she carefully skirted around it.

I shook my head as I dropped to my knees and pulled back the area rug. "Look!"

Joann and Kelly hurried over to see what I found. The faint outline indicated that the boards had been expertly cut.

"Is that a secret compartment?" Kelly asked.

"I think so," I answered as I traced the faint line, trying to dig out the floorboard pieces.

Joann placed a hand against one edge and the entire compartment tilted. My heart hammered against my ribs as I stared at the black, leather book housed inside.

The three of us grinned at each other as I pulled the book from its hiding spot and flipped it open.

"That's Alexander's handwriting," Joann said as she peered over the top of it.

"It looks like a journal. I wonder if he wrote about this party," I asked as I flipped to find the last entry.

"Did he?" Kelly asked.

My heart hammered harder against my ribs, my hands trembling. He did. "He did!"

My shaky finger trembled as I read the entry aloud that had been written only this morning. "Tonight, I host the party to end all parties. Ten guests, all of whom have some wrongdoing in their past. All of whom seem eager to keep their secret, otherwise, they wouldn't be coming. I expected this to be explosive. I also expect it to be lucrative. I hope to have at least ten million by the end of the night, though I wouldn't be surprised if I end up with more.

"I plan to play each of them against each other. That alone may double my haul. I do expect the threat of some violence, but I have invited a private investigator. If anything should happen, I will have her to rely upon to determine who is dangerous and who is not. I expect most will pay up with only one or two kicking up a fuss. But one can never be too careful...more later!"

I swallowed hard as I glanced at the other two ladies. "Those were his last words."

"So he was going to shake us down," Joann said with a shake of her head. "That's just like Alexander."

"Looks like he got more than he bargained for," I said with a shake of my head.

"And he expected you to figure out any issues," Kelly said, her hand falling on my shoulder. "So…this is all on you."

I heaved a sigh, shaking my head. "Yeah, thanks. No pressure."

"Well, you've already ruled out four people, so you're doing good so far."

"Five," I answered as I flipped backward to the entry before the last one.

Joann cocked her head. "Who else?"

"Edward," I said as I perused the writing on the page. "I think he's too tall for that knife wound. The angle is more straight on. If he stabbed Alexander, it would have been down from an angle. He's far taller than our host."

"Ohhh, wow, look at you go with the crime stuff," Kelly said before she snapped her gaze to Joann. "Right?"

"She's right. Alexander was short. Edward is far taller. The knife probably would've have been angled far more."

"Okay, good, so we've ruled out half of the people." Kelly bobbed her head.

I paged backward, reading a few of the entries. "It looks like all of the information shared earlier tonight is true. He mentions everything brought up in these earlier entries. He says something about proof."

"Probably in his safe," Joann said with a shake of her head. "I'm not sure I know the code."

"Can you try?" Kelly asked.

She shrugged. "I guess, but this may not work out."

"Doesn't matter," I said. "If we can find anything that could help us, it's worth a try. Except…we have to sneak back downstairs."

"Yep," Joann said as we all stood. "Well, I guess we'll try for it. Everyone remembers the way to the back stairs, right?"

Kelly and I nodded before we crossed to the door, all of us tense. My knees wobbled as Joann eased the door open.

"It's clear," she whispered before she darted into the hall and hurried down to the backstairs.

We raced along behind her before we pounded down the stairs, piling up at the bottom, breathless. My heart thudded in my chest as we waited at the door. If we were caught, would the killer strike again? Or would they turn the group against us, accusing us of being the murderers?

Joann inched the door open before she nodded. "Clear."

We hurried down the hall toward the office door, slipping inside without being caught. I blew out a long sigh of relief as Joann crossed to the safe.

She tried a few combinations, all of them failing.

"Try one, two, three, four," Kelly suggested.

Joann shot her a narrow-eyed glance before she returned her focus to the safe. After two more tries, a green light lit. "Got it!"

The door swung open, and I peered inside, my heart thudding hard.

Would we find anything inside that would help us figure out who the killer was?

CHAPTER 12

My breath caught in my throat as I stared into the interior of the safe. A thick folder sat in the middle, surrounded by a weapon and a few velvet boxes. Would the information inside this safe convict any of our remaining suspects, or would we only get more turned around?

With trembling fingers, I reached for the folder, withdrawing it as I held my breath. I plopped it on the desk as Kelly shined her flashlight on it, casting long shadows across the folder.

I grimaced at it, reminded of the blood pooled under Alexander Drake's chair in the dining room. "Of course he'd use a red folder."

"It's a red file. He kept them constantly in the office. Red files with things he could use against others to ensure successful business deals." Joann shook her head. "Then he decided to take it personal."

With a deep breath, I glanced from Joann to Kelly. "Are you sure you want to open this?"

"I'm sure. I know what's in there. Ledger entries showing I took the money, but I already explained that."

Joann nodded. "And mine I've explained, too. We need to focus on the five suspects we have left."

I nodded. "Right. Denise, Heather, Dawn, Tammy, and Pam. They are all still suspects."

We all focused on the folder as I flicked it open. My heart hammered as I grabbed the first stack of paper-clipped information.

"That's Edward," Kelly said, pointing to security footage of a man shaking hands with someone else.

"And that man he's meeting with facilitates insider trading in some of the highest profile cases," Joann said.

"Yes," I answered as I flipped to the next page, showing more evidence of his stock manipulation in the form of emails between Edward and his friends, discussing the timing of stock trades to maximize their values before the crash.

One of the emails urged the recipients to get out "before the bubble bursts," saying they didn't want to be "left holding the bag" when the thing went public.

"That's damning," Joann said as she read the email.

"And there's more," I said, my voice tight. I turned to the next set of documents—financial records. "Look at these transfers."

The records showed large sums of money being funneled into offshore accounts under names that were barely legible, but the dates matched the timing of the stock crash exactly. Edward had clearly been hedging his bets, ensuring he'd come out on top even as the market fell apart.

"And here," Kelly pointed to another document in the folder, "this is an internal memo from his company. It's about the stocks he was manipulating."

The memo hinted that Edward had access to confidential information about the stocks, advising others within the company to avoid certain investments, investments that Edward knew would fail.

"This is enough to ruin him," Joann whispered, her eyes wide. "If Alexander had this, he could've destroyed Edward's career."

"Or worse," I added, pulling out the final piece of the puzzle—a heavily redacted statement from a whistleblower within Edward's company. The witness detailed seeing Edward's involvement in the manipulation firsthand, enough to confirm everything in the folder. "Still, I think he's not our guy."

"I agree. Let's hope one of our remaining suspects has evidence like that so we can figure out who did this."

I flipped to the next set of papers in the folder, spotting a picture of Kelly on top. I swallowed hard, ready to bypass them when Kelly stopped me.

"Wait," she said, grabbing the papers, "I want to see what he has on me."

I swallowed hard, glancing sideways at her.

"What? I'll show it to you. I didn't do this," she said. She flipped through the evidence consisting of emails and pictures of in-person meetings as she tried to drum up support for her hostile takeover.

With a sigh, she tossed them down on the pile. "Dad would be devastated, but…I'd tell him to his face he's ruining the company."

There had been no other damning secrets in her file, so she seemed to be cleared. We found the evidence against Joann next, which was exactly what she'd said it would be: ledger entries showing the money being moved.

Evidence of Bonnie and Regina's secrets painted a grim

picture of the validity of their misdeeds, but since we'd already ruled them out, we moved on quickly after reviewing it.

My heart pounded harder as we finally reached one of our suspects.

I pulled out the clipped papers on Denise. The first page showed a formal complaint filed with the medical board detailing the botched surgery that had left a patient dead.

The paperwork claimed Denise had been under the influence of alcohol with several nurses reporting they'd smelled alcohol on her breath during the surgery.

An internal memo had been attached from the hospital administrator discussing a "private handling" of the situation to avoid public scandal.

Her medical license hadn't been suspended, but if this got out, she'd lose it for sure.

"She'd be ruined if that was made public," Kelly said.

"Yeah," I answered. "Definitely."

"So, she had motive to keep this quiet," Joann agreed.

I set the papers down on the right side of the desk. "There is our first suspect. Let's see if any of the others belong with her."

I picked up the next set of papers. "Heather's next."

We perused the proof detailing an investigation and valuation of pieces Heather had sold to various individuals. They were all deemed to be fake.

But even more damning than that were the private emails between Heather and a known art forger. Heather had amassed a small fortune selling all of these fake pieces. And all of it could be taken away from her if this got out.

Her entire career would be ruined, and she'd likely lose everything.

"Definitely a reason to kill," Kelly said. "She'd lose everything."

I dumped her folder into the suspect pile.

"Who's next?" Joann asked.

"Dawn. Let's see if her story checks out. Did she take a bribe or was she having an affair?"

I shuffled through the papers, finding several photographs of Dawn with a man who was not her husband. I continued in search of any signs of bribery or corruption but found none.

Dawn had told the truth earlier. Her story had been infidelity, nothing more.

"She told us all this," Kelly said with a shrug. "Do you think she still had a motive?"

I stared down at the file for a moment before I dumped it on the left side of the desk, clearing her.

"Two left. Next up is Tammy," I said.

At the top of the stack of papers was the article in question, Children of War. It had been highlighted and annotated with numerous inconsistencies. All of them had been vetted through fact checkers to prove they were manipulated.

A report from an independent auditor confirmed that the children featured in the article did not come from the war-torn country Tammy had claimed. Instead, they were models hired from a local agency. Emails between Tammy and her editor suggested that she had been under immense pressure to produce a groundbreaking story, leading her to fabricate the details.

"Wow, so she made up her award-winning story," Kelly said.

"Yep, and this is career-ending stuff. I'd say she could be guilty," Kelly said.

I nodded and placed the file with the other two.

Three suspects, one more to vet through. I picked up Pam's folder and dove into the materials.

Pam had maintained her innocence, claiming her actions

were part of standard scientific protocols, but the rumors painted a much darker picture.

The first document was a complaint filed by a group of patients who had participated in one of Pam's clinical trials. They alleged that she had knowingly withheld treatment from them, giving them placebos instead of the actual medication they had been promised. The result had been disastrous for some: severe complications, even death.

As I read further, I found internal memos from the pharmaceutical company Pam had worked with. These memos revealed that Pam had indeed been instructed to conduct the trial as ethically as possible, but she chose to manipulate the data to produce more dramatic results. The memos also included exchanges where she expressed concerns about the trial's progress, but instead of addressing these issues ethically, she decided to push forward, sacrificing the well-being of her patients to ensure the trial's success.

"Wow," Joann murmured. "Look at that. She's another one who could lose everything."

With a nod from Kelly, I dumped her file with the other three. Four suspects remained. I wondered how we'd vet through the evidence. Would anything point to someone specific?

"What's this?" Kelly asked as she picked up a crinkled paper from the bottom of the folder.

I narrowed my eyes at it. A hastily scrawled note, smudged and crumpled, had been carefully saved.

Joann read it aloud as the long shadows in the room seemed to grow longer. "*Alexander. It's getting harder to breathe under all this weight. I know what you hold over me, and I'm willing to do what it takes to keep this story buried. This ends now...one way or another.*"

"It's not signed," Kelly said, "so it doesn't help."

I stared at it, my lips parted. I stared at the letter, my heart racing as the pieces finally clicked into place. The truth was staring me in the face, and with it, a chilling realization. "Actually, it does. I know who did this. I know who killed him."

CHAPTER 13

I stared at the four folders spread out on the right side of the desk. One of those people was a murderer, and I knew which one it was. My heart rose into my throat as all the pieces of the puzzle fell into place. From the way she'd carefully guided the conversation earlier, staying quiet in critical moments and speaking up when she needed to, down to the motive clearly hinted at in the threatening note we'd found at the bottom of the evidence folder, her guilt screamed at me.

"You know?" Kelly asked her nose wrinkling.

I bobbed my head, my throat parching as I realized how close I'd been to a woman who was capable of murdering someone to keep her secret.

"Who is it?" Kelly asked before she sliced a hand through the air. "Wait, don't tell me. I know! It's Heather, isn't it? Never trust a woman named Heather."

I shook my head. "No, it's not Heather."

"Denise?" Kelly questioned.

"Definitely not," Joann said, crossing her arms.

"Who?" Kelly asked. "I feel so dumb."

I poked a finger at the words in the threatening note.

"Keep this story buried?" Kelly cocked her head, her eyebrows pinching.

"Who else would say that but a journalist?" Joann answered.

I nodded. "What she said. This has to be Tammy. Think about it."

"I have," Joann answered. "She pointed the finger at everyone else when the secrets came out but stayed relatively quiet herself. And that last clue did it in for me."

I poked a finger at my compatriot. "Exactly. Tammy did it. Tammy is our killer!"

"You got that right," a new voice growled from the doorway.

I snapped my gaze in its direction as Kelly flicked her flashlight toward the door. We all gasped, spotting Tammy with my handgun pointed at us.

My eyes widened, my stomach twisting into a tight knot. We should have gone to my room to retrieve that before we'd searched for clues.

"Tammy!" Kelly exclaimed. "What are you doing here?"

"Searching for the evidence that paints me as the guilty party so I can destroy it."

I grabbed the packet of information and the damning letter and shoved it behind my back. "I don't think so."

Tammy arched an eyebrow at me. "And how do you think you're going to stop me? Hmm?"

I shrugged as I refused to budge. "I'm going to…I'll think of something."

"I'm going to kill you and take it. And I'll kill anyone else who tries to stop me, too," Tammy snarled.

Joann raced to the side of the room, stretching her arms out. "Throw it!"

As Tammy aimed her weapon, I tossed the paperwork to

Joann. She caught it midair. Tammy tried to recalibrate, swinging the weapon to Joann when she flung the paperwork in Kelly's direction.

"Ah!" Kelly shouted as she stumbled forward to grab it and hurry to another spot in the room.

"Charlie! Catch!" Kelly flung the papers at me as I ran to another location.

We continued tossing the papers around and flitting to new areas in the room with Tammy flailing around with the gun in a desperate chase.

My chest heaved as I started to get winded. I wasn't certain how much longer I could keep this up. And we hadn't found a way out of the room yet.

We were trapped by the gun-toting woman at the door no matter how much we ran around.

I caught the papers again and tossed them over to Joann as she dashed by me. The game continued, with Joann throwing them to Kelly and Kelly returning them to me when a loud noise deafened me.

My eyes widened at the gunshot, and I first glanced down at my own body before I checked Kelly and Joann. Everyone seemed intact.

I cut my gaze to Tammy, spotting the gun pointed in the air. She'd fired a bullet just to get our attention, but now she looked ready for business. She lowered the weapon, pointing it directly at me.

"Enough with these games. Give me those papers, or I'll kill you."

"You'll have to kill me, then. Because I'm not giving them up," I said, raising my chin.

I thrust them behind my back, my heart hammering as I wondered if she would shoot me point blank.

Joann stepped in front of me. "You'll have to go through me, too."

Kelly scurried over, getting between me and Joann. "And me…me second, though. After Joann."

I crinkled my brow at the odd statement, though I appreciated her support whether it was second or first. I wasn't certain how Joann felt.

"Fine. I'll kill all of you. Doesn't matter to me. It's Charlie's gun. I'll set it up to look like a murder-suicide."

My throat parched as Tammy slid the gun forward, her finger tightening on the trigger. I braced myself for the sound of the gun firing, the sound of Joann's body slumping to the floor.

Just as Tammy's finger tightened on the trigger, a blur of movement caught my eye. Denise charged forward with a bookend, bringing it down with a sickening thud. Tammy crumpled to the ground, the gun still clutched in her hand. We stood there, breathless, the room eerily silent except for the pounding of my heart.

Denise stared at us for a moment before she adjusted her sleeve as she lowered her arm. "Looked like you ladies could have used some help."

I swallowed hard, trying to wet my dry throat. "W-we did, yeah," I said. "Tammy is the killer."

Denise glanced down at the unconscious woman as Kelly pried my gun away from her fingers and handed it back to me.

"I gathered as much. And…" Denise pulled a phone from her pocket, showing us a recording. "I recorded her confession."

"Amazing," I said, a smile curling my lips. "Great work."

Denise bobbed her head as she shoved her phone into her pocket.

"Now," I answered, "we should…tie her up or something. Until we can get off this island."

Joann grabbed one of the cords holding the drapes back

and wound it around Tammy's wrists before she could awaken.

I'd caught my first killer and solved my first case. I couldn't wait to get off the island, but still…at least we could all sleep a little better now knowing a murderer didn't walk free among us.

* * *

Bright sunshine shone through the glass floating high above the foyer. I crossed my arms as I explained the evidence to the officer who had responded to the help call the butler made once the storm passed.

They didn't get to us for hours, but we took turns watching our perp to make certain she didn't escape and cause more problems.

As the police hauled her way, with her yammering on about her innocence and how we'd framed her, the rest of the group gathered in the foyer.

As I watched Tammy being led away in handcuffs, a wave of relief washed over me. I had solved my first big case, but the adrenaline still pumped through my veins. The weight of what could have happened, of how close we all came to becoming victims, lingered in the back of my mind. But with that fear came a newfound determination. This was just the beginning.

"Well," I said as I rolled my bag closer, "I wish I could say it's been fun but…that hasn't really been the case."

"But you did solve your first big case," Joann said with a warm smile.

I bobbed my head. "I did. And I'm pretty proud of that."

I leaned forward and unzipped the front flap of my suitcase, tugging out a thick folder. "And on top of that, I found all of the evidence of the secrets you all kept."

I shook my head as I looked down at them, noting the uncomfortable faces surrounding me. With a flick of my finger, I opened the folder and distributed all of the proof to each person. Their secrets were their own to keep.

Denise stared down at hers before she strode into the living room where the butler had kept the fire roaring for us overnight. She tossed hers inside and dusted her hands. "I'm not keeping that. I'm turning over a new leaf. Moving on."

"To?" I asked.

Denise lifted her chin. "I'm going to write murder mysteries."

The others followed behind her, each of them tossing the evidence into the flames. Regina spun to face the others. "I'm moving on, too. To producing. And I'm going to cast Olivia Green as my lead."

I smiled at the gesture as Bonnie heaved a sigh. "I'm changing, too. Writing isn't for me. But I can edit. I'm going to edit someone's next bestseller."

"And I," Heather said, "am no longer selling art. I'm going to make it. I'm going to go back to sculpting my own pieces."

Expressions of best wishes floated from the others before Dawn spoke up. "This has changed me too. Outside of devoting my life to my family, I'm going to investigate politicians who are corrupt and make sure they are ousted."

The others nodded and smiled at the idea before Pam flicked a lock of her blonde hair away from her face. "And I am joining an oversight committee to keep a watch on scientific experiments."

Edward cleared his throat as he watched the edges of his paper burn. "I'm leaving banking and finance to open my own business. I'm going to hunt for the next big business idea and back them."

Kelly chuckled. "You and I should talk. I'm not going to

worry about Culpepper Enterprises anymore. I'm going my own way. Opening a new kitchenware company."

"And I am looking to invest, too. Maybe the three of us can chat," Joann answered.

It seemed everyone had found a new way forward in life. While the weekend hadn't been what Alexander Drake expected, it had a profound effect on his guests.

As for me, I was going to use this case as my jumping off point to be the best private investigator the world had ever seen.

As I wheeled my suitcase down the path to the boat, the island slowly receding behind me, I couldn't help but glance back one last time. This place had held danger and secrets, but it had also marked the beginning of something new. I was no longer just Charlie—I was Charlie, the private investigator, ready to take on whatever came next.

Want another great murder mystery read? Check out *Murder of Pearl* to help the Silverman sisters solve a murder at their pearl party event!

Claim your five free books now! Join my newsletter!

ABOUT THE AUTHOR

Award-winning author Nellie H. Steele writes in as many genres as she reads, ranging from mystery to fantasy and allowing readers to escape reality and enter enchanting worlds filled with unique, lovable characters.

Addicted to books since she could read, Nellie escaped to fictional worlds like the ones created by Carolyn Keene or Victoria Holt long before she decided to put pen to paper and create her own realities.

When she's not spinning a cozy mystery tale, building a new realm in a contemporary fantasy, or writing another action-adventure car chase, you can find her shuffling through her Noah's Ark of rescue animals or enjoying a hot cuppa (that's tea for most Americans.)

Join her Facebook Readers' Group here!

SERIES BY NELLIE H. STEELE

Cate Kensie Mysteries

Shadow Slayers Stories

Lily & Cassie by the Sea Mysteries

Great Maine Mysteries

Pearl Party Mysteries

Middle Age is Murder Cozy Mysteries

Duchess of Blackmoore Mysteries

Shadow Lake Ranch Murders

Maggie Edwards Adventures

Clif & Ri on the Sea Adventures

Shelving Magic

Affair with Hair Cozy Mysteries